MURKY PASSIONS AND SCANDALS

A RAINA SUN MYSTERY

ANNE R. TAN

To Red,
my childhood wouldn't have been the same without you.

SUPER FREAK

Raina Sun knew she'd made a tactical error two minutes into the surveillance job for Moody Investigation's newest client. She'd asked her grandma to keep her company in this easy assignment. Since seven o'clock in the morning, Raina and Po Po had watched the Westchester home, a ten-thousand-square-foot monstrosity, from the comfort of Raina's thirteen-year-old car. It was only a quarter past nine, and she was ready to strangle her grandma.

Po Po popped the top of her second can of Red Bull. "How much longer will this take? Maybe we should barge into the home and rough her up a bit to get a confession."

Her grandma didn't need the caffeine. At seventy—wait, her grandma was sixty this week—and a little over five feet, Po Po was a ball of energy. Ever since they got back to California from Toronto a few months ago, her grandma had an extra spring in her step and more bounce in her hair—literally, since she turned her long silvery braid into a chin-length bob with pink streaks.

Raina rubbed her temple. This was the third outrageous suggestion in the last fifteen minutes. "There's no confession. We're only noting her activities while her husband is at work. There might not even be an affair."

"Of course there's an affair. First, he's old and rich," Po Po said, ticking the point off on her fingers. "She's young enough to be his granddaughter—"

"He's not old. He's only in his late fifties—"

"He probably needs to stock the little blue pill like toilet paper to keep her happy. It's that Latina blood. I bet you they have a fireman pole in the bedroom—"

Raina plugged her fingers into her ears. "La-la-la."

Po Po threw her hands up in the air. "You'll be a married woman soon. You need to hear these things so you can keep your man happy."

Raina sighed. If Matthew wanted a pole in their bedroom, she would tell him exactly where to put it. "Why don't we play the Quiet Game? The first person to speak loses." She mimed zipping up her lips and tossing away the key. Sometimes a kindergartner was more obliging than her grandma.

Po Po gave her an expression that said she was only biding her time. She rooted inside her large hobo bag that could double for a carry-on and probably held weapons of mass destruction. She pulled out her cell phone and tapped on the screen. Blessed silence filled the faded red Honda.

The surveillance job was Raina's first assignment without supervision. Sure it was minimum wage, but the hours counted as paid experience toward a private investigator license. It was simple enough to tail the client's third wife and document her affair. A little sleazy, yes, but it was much safer than a murder investigation.

Po Po held out her cell phone. "Your sister wants to talk to you."

Raina shook her head. "Not now. I'm on the job."

"You're not doing anything at the moment. She wants your help."

"I don't want to get in the middle of their marriage. If she wants to know what's going on with her husband, she should ask him."

Po Po's fingers flew across the screen, tapping out a text. Her phone chirped at the incoming message. "She said she'd pay you to play detective."

"I don't need her to pay me. I already have a job as a detective," Raina said. She sounded peevish, and she didn't like it. Her older sister always had a way of getting under her skin.

"She said—"

"Something is happening." Raina started her car and reached for her seatbelt. "Tell Cassie we'll get back to her later."

The carriage-style garage door of the McMansion rolled open, and a stunning Hispanic woman in her early thirties drove out in a black Mercedes-Benz SUV. Even from a distance, Raina could see the wide brown eyes and kissable pouty mouth on the oval face meant for a magazine. Some women had all the luck.

Not that Raina was jealous. After all, the curly black hair that made her look like a walking cotton candy on a stick was good enough to get her Matthew. And old age would add enough padding to her boyish figure, although it probably wouldn't be at desirable locations.

She snorted. Who was she kidding? Of course, she was slightly jealous, but it would all even out. In fifty years, time and gravity would make both of them look like the cute apple head dolls found at craft fairs.

Besides, there was trouble in paradise. Mia Westchester's husband wouldn't have hired a private investigator to tail her if all was well at the home front. She made a left out of the driveway and came toward them.

Raina flipped the visor down and pretended to check non-existent eye makeup in the mirror, partially blocking her face with her hand. Po Po ducked, squeezing her head between her knees. Mia paid them no attention and kept going. When the coast was clear, Raina signaled and made a U-turn to follow their quarry.

Po Po made a fist pump and bounced on her seat. "Showtime!"

"The husband only wants to document where she's going while he's at work. I don't think she's doing anything all that exciting," Raina said, secretly hoping she was wrong. The last few days had been a snooze fest.

"Hot and steamy! Hot and steamy!" Po Po chanted like a child wishing for a treat. "I hope she's doing the nasty with the cabana boy."

Raina wanted to slam her head on the steering wheel. Why did she think it was a good idea to include her grandma? Oh, right. So Po Po wouldn't feel neglected now that she had to share Raina's time with Matthew. Talk about juggling two big babies.

Five minutes later the SUV pulled into the parking lot of a medical office complex.

"See? She probably has a doctor's appointment," Raina said.

Po Po slumped back in her seat, disappointment written across her face.

Raina slowed and rolled past the driveway for a street side parking spot. From the rear view mirror, she saw a white van with dark windows pull up next to the SUV.

"Come on, cabana boy," Po Po said, twisting her upper body to look out the rear window. "Hey! A three-some. Oh, she's a super freak. I like her already."

Raina pulled up next to the curb, thankful she didn't have to deal with parallel parking. She whipped around to see what her grandma was crowing about.

Two Hispanic men with dark sunglasses and full beards—scruffy and definitely not cabana boy caliber —came out of the white van. They opened the SUV driver door and pulled the wife out of the vehicle. She screamed and threw a punch, but one man pinned her arms behind her.

"What's going on?" Po Po said, her voice full of alarm. "We have to do something."

Raina threw off her seatbelt and grabbed the pepper spray from her purse. "Call the police. She's being kidnapped," she called over her shoulder. She took off toward the van.

One man held the woman against his chest, and the other pressed a rag against her mouth. Within seconds she sagged and went limp. They tossed her effortlessly into the van and slammed the door shut.

The van driver pulled out of the parking lot, nearly plowing into a car pulling into the lot. The car's driver honked and cursed at the white van. The van driver gave him the bird and peeled out of the parking lot in a squeal of tires.

Raina pumped her arms and pushed a little harder. Even though she was in decent shape, she couldn't outrun a speeding vehicle. Her lungs burned, and her breath came out in loud puffs.

"Duck!" Po Po hollered from behind.

Raina dropped to the ground.

Wha-amp! Wha-amp!

Air rushed past Raina. She lifted her head to see mini pumpkins smacking into the bumper and splattering onto the road. The white van swayed into oncoming traffic and over-corrected itself, sideswiping the parked vehicles.

Wha-amp!

The mini pumpkin missed its target, hit the parked green car by the curb, and splattered onto the road.

The white van hooked a right and disappeared from view.

Raina got up and jogged back to her grandma. Po Po lowered a small cylindrical metal tube from her shoulder. Where did her grandma get the homemade pumpkin launcher? And how did she fit it into her bag?

"In the car. Let's go," Raina said, hopping in and turning on the engine. She made an illegal U-turn and chased after the white van, taking the right turn too wide for her comfort.

Po Po held onto the handle above the window, the pumpkin launcher cradled between her knees. With her other hand, she dug out her bird watching binoculars from her purse. "Six. Alpha. Foxtrot. Papa. One. Four. Two," she called out the license plate's numbers. "I'll memorize the letters, and you'll memorize the numbers."

Raina nodded. "Okay. One-two-four."

"One-four-two," Po Po corrected, tossing the binoculars back into her bag. She leaned out the window and settled the pumpkin launcher between her shoulder and ear.

"What do you think you're doing?" Raina said, reaching across the center console to hold onto the elastic waistband of her grandma's jeans. "Sit down, Po Po. You'll fall out of the car, and I can't drive with one hand holding onto your behind."

"Just give me one shot." Her grandma aimed and

pulled the trigger. A mini pumpkin launched out of the tube and missed the van.

The van driver slammed on the brakes and hooked a left, almost getting into a head-on collision with traffic from the opposite lane.

Raina pulled up to the next intersection to make a legal U-turn. By the time she got to the street where she'd last seen the white van, it was long gone—along with the woman she was paid to tail.

WHEN RAINA and Po Po returned to the crime scene, they found Officer Joanna Hopper pacing the parking lot, inspecting the asphalt. Her police cruiser was parked next to the curb behind the green car with a dent from the pumpkin launcher. If they squinted, the golf ball-size dent wasn't noticeable.

"How are we to explain the mini pumpkins? Do we need to leave our insurance information for the green car?" Raina asked her grandma.

Po Po tucked the pumpkin launcher back into her purse. She put a finger to her lips. "Shhhh. No one has to know. Collateral damage is to be expected."

"But what about the green car?"

Po Po pulled out an envelope from her purse and waved it in the air. "There's enough money in here to cover the damage. Spillman Insurance is helping me find a new umbrella policy. The last one canceled mine." She rolled her eyes. "Apparently I put in too many claims."

"But shouldn't we at least leave a note with the money?"

"Got that covered too. There's a canned letter inside, apologizing for the damage, and some cash to cover the repair bill." Po Po beamed. "Am I smart or what?"

Raina ignored the question. It was a fantastic solution to an awkward situation. No name and phone numbers to leave behind. But what little old granny walked around with pre-written apology notes and cash in an envelope? "How many of these envelopes do you have in your purse?"

"Not that many. I'm down to one now. I'll have to get back to the condo soon so I can replenish."

"Po Po, is it safe to be walking around with this much money?"

"It's just a temporary solution until I can get another policy. I have full faith in Spillman Insurance." Po Po tucked the envelope back inside her purse. "I'll leave the note after the policewoman leaves. I don't want her asking questions. I'm not sure my new toy is, uh...legal."

Raina groaned inwardly. She didn't even want to start on the subject of legality with her grandma. "Where did you get it?"

"The high school kids built it for me. I offered a five-hundred-dollar scholarship to the team who could make it small enough to fit into my bag."

Raina could imagine what the family would say if her grandma got hauled into the police station for corrupting the youths in town. "We better go over to Officer Hopper before she comes over here. I don't want her to see your new toy."

They got out of Raina's faded red Honda Accord and trotted toward the officer. People came out of the office building and got into their cars, probably going out for lunch. Surprisingly, they only gave Officer Hopper a passing glance.

"The only suspicious thing I see is the splattered mini pumpkin on the street," Officer Hopper said, hands on her hips. She was older than Raina, probably thirty years old. Her blonde hair was pulled back in a tight French braid, and her flinty gray eyes regarded the two of them like they were a couple of pranksters.

Raina gave her grandma a sideways glance. Po Po put on her best senile senior citizen look, her eyes at half-mast and unfocused. At moments like this, Raina wanted nothing more than to call her grandma out.

Suppressing a sigh, Raina addressed the police officer. "We saw a woman get kidnapped in this parking lot. Her name is Mia Westchester."

"Is this a joke?" Officer Hopper said, glancing at Po Po. "This is not the first time the senior citizens in this town have led me on a wild goose chase."

Po Po blinked like she wasn't the ringleader for these previous operations to get even with the officer who was once Raina's romantic rival. "We have the license plate number for the van." She rattled it off.

Officer Hopper pulled out a notebook and wrote down the license plate number. "I'll run this through the system." Her tone sounded bored like she was indulging them.

Raina walked over to Mia's car and glanced inside. The keys dangled from the ignition, and her purse was in the passenger seat. "If she wasn't kidnapped, how do you explain her keys and purse in the car?"

Officer Hopper came over and glanced inside. Her expression morphed from annoyance to alarm. "I'm calling for backup."

The next two hours flew by in a blur. They were questioned and re-questioned, more police officers came and went, walkie-talkies crackled with life and fell into silence, and her grandma complained about missing lunch. They were finally thanked for their time and dismissed. In other words, the police would take over from here.

Raina and Po Po headed for the Venus Café. Depending on who you talked to in town, the café was either a welcoming gathering place or an abomination. It was unassuming on the outside—an olive green bungalow with white trim—but like everything else in life, it was the inside that showed the world who you really were.

The Venus Café had floor-to-ceiling murals of handsome men frolicking with the Greek goddess in the woods. Only strategically placed flowing hair or bits of leaves kept the paintings in the art category. Raina always felt a secret thrill when she stepped into the café. It was good to be a little naughty even if it was vicariously through painted women.

It was two thirty, which meant the senior citizen crowd would be drifting in for the early bird dinner soon. One of Po Po's friends was already there, reading in a cracked leather chair by the large fireplace.

Brenda Sullivan, the owner, was wiping a table when they came in. "Your usual?" she asked, pulling a notepad from the pocket of her apron.

"I am so hungry I could eat my foot. No senior portion for me this time," Po Po said, dropping into a chair at the adjacent table.

The café owner raised an eyebrow and glanced at Raina. "Difficult morning?"

"You can say that again. There was a kidnapping, and then we got into a high-speed car chase," Po Po said. She took a deep breath. "And—"

"A roast beef sandwich on sourdough and a large ice caramel macchiato," Raina cut in. "Please put our order in the kitchen first."

Brenda tore the order slip from the notepad and headed toward the kitchen. "I'll be right back." Half a minute later she settled herself across from Po Po. "So who got kidnapped?"

As Raina listened to her grandma launch into the tale, an uneasy feeling settled in her stomach that had nothing to do with food. The three of them had discussed other cases in the past, but this Westchester case was different. Even though Raina trusted Brenda to not talk about this case with anyone else, she was still breaching a client's privacy.

What if she could no longer discuss her cases with anyone? She didn't think being a private detective meant she would end up a lone wolf seeking justice for her clients. This private investigator business was more complicated than she had envisioned.

Her grandma mimed using her homemade pumpkin launcher. "And then—"

"Brenda," Raina interrupted. "Could you pack my lunch to go? I need to get back to the office." As long as she wasn't here, she technically wasn't discussing her client's case. Besides, she should probably tell her boss about the kidnapping before she heard it from someone else.

"Do you want me to go with you?" Po Po asked. Her tone implied she was only asking out of politeness.

Raina shook her head. She knew her grandma couldn't wait to get back to the senior center to tell her cronies about her great escapade this morning. "I'll probably have to file a report and call our client."

"What are you going to tell the husband?" Brenda asked.

"I don't know. It depends on whether or not the police called him yet," Raina said.

"What are you going to tell your new boss?" Po Po asked.

Raina grimaced. "I don't know."

"Well, at least she can't blame you for this," Brenda

said. "It's not like you had anything to do with the kidnapping."

While Raina might've had nothing to do with the kidnapping, she couldn't help but worry about Arthur Westchester's reaction when he found out his wife was kidnapped right in front of Raina's eyes.

2

FROM BAD TO WORSE

Moody Investigation was in the same office building as the town's newspaper, *Gold Springs Weekly*. Raina hadn't known there was a private investigation office in the basement until three weeks ago when she started the job. The drive took less than five minutes, but she sat in the parking lot for another ten minutes, inhaling her sandwich. She might not have a chance to eat once inside.

The inner office door was closed when Raina strolled into the office. Her boss must be with a client. There was nothing exciting about the space—no large bulletin boards with clues pinned to it or high-tech spy equipment. Without the black lettering on the glass door announcing their business, the room looked just like any nondescript office suite with its white walls, tan carpet, and cheap beige furniture.

Raina dropped her purse on the desk that doubled

as a receptionist counter. She grabbed the key to open the locked filing cabinet behind her and got the file for Arthur Westchester.

The business tycoon, a well-known developer who made his fortune from purchasing cheap land and building dense subdivisions, came in earlier in the week. He plunked down a thousand-dollar retainer and asked for a report on his young wife's weekly activities while he was in the office.

Toni Moody had shown Raina the ropes on how to do a surveillance the first two days, and then she'd turned the case over to Raina. For three days, Raina had followed Mia Westchester around town and even to her shopping trip in Sacramento. Easy peasy—until this morning.

Raina and her boss had a bet on whether the Westchesters were heading toward divorce court. Twice divorced herself, Toni was convinced Arthur wanted proof of his wife's infidelity to reduce his alimony payments. Raina thought he wanted proof his wife still loved him. But after this morning, she wondered if their investigation might take a different course.

The inner door clicked open, and Toni Moody and Arthur Westchester came out of the inner office. The conversation trailed off, and both of them glared at Raina.

For a man whose wife just got kidnapped, Arthur looked more annoyed than worried. With the cuffs of his sleeves rolled up on his pinstriped shirt and disarrayed blond toupee, he looked every bit like a harried businessman. Raina wondered what meeting he'd missed to be here.

Arthur took a deep breath and shook off his dark mood visibly. He glanced at Raina. "You're still young, and someday you might do some good in this world. But lying to get attention is the wrong path to take."

Raina swallowed, her stomach fluttering with a sense of foreboding. What lies was he talking about? What was going on here? She glanced over at Toni to gauge her reaction. Her boss ignored her.

Arthur shook Toni's hand and said, "Thank you for understanding, Ms. Moody. I can see myself out."

After he left, the silence in the office stretched until Raina squirmed in her seat. Her new boss studied her from the doorway as if weighing her worth.

Toni Moody's dark brown face gave nothing away. Tall and rotund, her boss was a formidable woman. She wouldn't have lasted in this profession otherwise. Her long silver braid didn't soften her features one bit.

Raina cleared her throat. "We need to talk about Mr. Westchester's wife. She was kidnapped this morning."

Toni raised an eyebrow. "Tell me what happened."

Raina didn't like the sound of this. Did she do something wrong? Having her grandma with her shouldn't be this big of a deal, right? She told her boss about the kidnapping but left out the detail of the pumpkin launcher.

Toni's body language didn't change, but something

shifted in her eyes by the end of the tale. "And your grandmother was with you the entire time?" Her question seemed heavy with hidden meaning.

Raina nodded. "I'm sorry if this is against company policy. I haven't been spending time with her—"

Toni waved dismissively. "I'm not worried about your grandmother. What concerned me is that Arthur Westchester came in piping mad because the police showed up in his office."

"I don't understand. Why wouldn't he want to know his wife got kidnapped?"

"Because she didn't get abducted. Mia Westchester was at the day spa with her mother this morning."

Raina's mouth dropped open. What! "Does Mia Westchester have a twin? I didn't follow the wrong woman. I'm not incompetent."

"I didn't say you were, but our client just fired us."

"Does he think my grandma and I made the whole thing up? Why would we do something like this?"

"I don't know what he's thinking, but I can't afford to lose clients. You should've called me first before calling the police."

"If I'd called you first, how would things play out differently?" Raina asked, hoping she didn't sound like she was challenging her boss's authority. It would've been a waste of time to call her boss and then call the police.

"No, it wouldn't be any different. I hired you because you have good instincts." Toni sighed. "This supposed kidnapping is a complication I don't need."

"Do you want me to check on the wife?" Raina asked. "Maybe I could ask her a few questions to see if she is lying."

Toni shook her head. "As far as I'm concerned, we're off the case. I need to worry about billable hours if I'm to pay you this week. Did you finish typing up the report for the pie lady's case?"

"I'm halfway through. I'll finish up before I leave today. I can't believe you found out her sister-in-law was selling her proprietary pie recipes. I always stop by Peaches Pies whenever I'm in that part of town."

"Being a PI isn't always glamorous. I was hip deep in pig shit at the end—literally."

Raina chuckled, appreciating her boss's attempt to lighten the mood. She didn't appreciate looking like an incompetent fool in front of her boss. If Toni Moody decided she no longer needed an intern, Raina would have to find a firm in Sacramento to take her on to get the required professional hours to get her private investigator license. She shouldn't risk upsetting her boss to satisfy her curiosity.

She spent the next hour writing up the report, but the Westchester case kept nagging her. Something was going down in the Westchester household, and somebody was lying in the family. Her bet was on the wife.

AFTER RAINA GOT OFF WORK, she swung by the exclusive Inner Beauty Day Spa in Gold Springs' historic downtown. The other day spas within a ten-mile radius had a different clientele, and Raina couldn't see a woman like Mia Westchester slumming it.

The bell on the glass door chimed when Raina opened the door of the day spa. The small front area looked much like it did when she worked here earlier in the year—a minimalist decor with natural light coming in from the glass front windows. There was one loveseat, a potted plant, and the receptionist counter. The rest of the spa was hidden behind a beaded curtain.

Raina asked the receptionist for Myra Jo Landon even though she had no appointment. She'd helped the spa owner out of a jam once, so she wasn't worried about being turned away. The receptionist spoke on the phone and waved Raina through. She strode through the beaded curtain, ignoring the robed women in the lounge, to Myra Jo's office and knocked on the door.

The petite spa owner got up and gestured at a chair. "Raina, what a lovely surprise. Please shut the door behind you."

Her smile didn't match the wariness behind her blue eyes. She was probably expecting trouble to follow in Raina's shadow. She was shorter and heavier than Raina, but she radiated an earth motherly vibe that Raina would never be able to imitate.

"Assuming you're not here to apply for a job, how can I help you?" Myra Jo asked, settling back in the chair behind the battered desk.

"Was Mia Westchester at the spa this morning?" Raina asked.

"Answering you would be a breach of my client's privacy."

Raina gave her an apologetic shrug. "I'm sorry to put you in this situation, but if I don't find out about Mia's whereabouts this morning, I could get fired from my new job. Then I would have to try to get a job here...again." A small reminder of the favor the Landon family owed her.

Myra Jo studied Raina. Several seconds ticked by before she said, "Can I ask what this is about?"

"You could, but then you either have to self-destruct or I will have to do something about it," Raina said, smiling at the ridiculous image of Myra Jo exploding like an overstuffed chicken.

The spa owner's expression didn't change, and she sighed like Raina needed her head examined. But she tilted the monitor so both of them could see the screen. A few taps on the keyboard and the appointment calendar popped up on the screen.

"Yes, she was here for a sixty-minute massage," Myra Jo said.

"What time was this?"

"Eleven-thirty."

Raina tapped her fingers on her thighs, considering what the spa owner just said. The kidnapping took place around nine-thirty in the morning, but Mia Westchester didn't show up to the day spa until eleven-thirty. Two hours were unaccounted for. "Was she by herself?"

Myra Jo glanced at the screen again. "The appointment was for a two-person massage. The masseuse would know more, but I can't allow you to talk to her."

Raina shook her head. There was no need to speak with the masseuse. Since Mia Westchester told the police and her husband she was with her mother, it would check out. "Was this a pre-scheduled appointment?"

"It was a walk-in," Myra Jo said.

Raina thanked the spa owner for trusting her with the information and left. As she drove back to her apartment, she ran through the timeline in her head again. Even if Mia had to pick up her mother, there was still time for something to happen between her and the kidnappers.

So what happened in those two hours, and why did she lie? Was she trying to protect the kidnappers? This would imply she knew them. But if she knew them, then why did she get kidnapped?

Raina rubbed her temples on her way back to her car. This was too convoluted. Their client had fired them from the job, so there was no reason for her to keep digging...except she couldn't get rid of the unease in her stomach.

If Arthur Westchester hadn't shown up at the office, she might have been able to let this case go. But as it stood now, she would have to get to the bottom of this supposed kidnapping because she refused to start a new profession with this hanging over her head. While she had no problem with looking foolish, she had a problem with someone calling her a liar.

WHEN RAINA WALKED through the front door of her apartment, she found her fiancé sitting on her sofa with a beer can in one hand and flipping through the channels on the TV. They hadn't broached the subject of their living arrangement or even set a date for the wedding. The engagement was still too new, but Raina had hoped they would have made more progress than unannounced dinner dates.

"I'm surprised you still have your pants on, and your hand on the remote," Raina said dryly.

Matthew Louie glanced over at her, his gold-flecked brown eyes twinkling with amusement. "If you want my pants off, all you gotta do is ask, Rainy."

She snorted and dropped her purse on the small side table by the front door. An incident earlier in the year left a hole in the drywall next to the table, but a potted plant hid the patch job.

"So did you show up with dinner, or were you hoping I'll make you dinner?" Her tone implied he better choose his words carefully. If he thought the sudden change in their relationship status meant he got a personal chef at his beck and call, he was in for a surprise.

He settled on *Sherlock*. "The pizza is in the oven. I

figured you'd want it warm. Do you want to eat now?"

"Give me a few minutes to change into something more comfortable?"

He gave her a lopsided grin that made her insides all gooey. "Want me to help?"

"I want dinner before the pizza turns into a hard disc in the oven."

He shrugged as if to say it was her loss, which was probably true. "How did your date go with your grandmother?"

Matthew had encouraged her to take Po Po with her on the surveillance job because her grandma needed cheering up. If Raina hadn't known he was Mr. Right already, this alone would have done it.

He thought it was the tedium of small town living and petty offenses at the senior center that made her grandma snappish around him lately. Raina didn't have the heart to tell him that her grandma was jealous of him. She wasn't used to having to share Raina's time.

"You didn't hear about my bogus kidnapping call? I thought Officer Hopper would've told you about this at the station."

Matthew was a homicide detective for the Gold Springs Police Department, and he seemed to have a way of keeping track of her movements around town. She hoped he didn't get too big of a ribbing from the guys. The last thing she needed was to have a reputation for jumping to conclusions at the police station before they even got married.

He made a face. "I was working on the budget with

the chief. I can't wait until my boss comes back from medical leave. So what happened?"

She told him about her day.

"So that was why Joanna gave me the stink eye," Matthew said. "I wonder if the other guys made fun of her for believing you."

"Do you think I made the whole thing up?"

He held up both hands, palms facing her. "You're not the type to overreact. Something's fishy about this, but I don't have time to look into it. I was volun-teered"—he made air quotes with his fingers—"as tribute to finish up a two-week training course the department already paid for. I'll have to drive to Cuper-tino in the morning."

This would give Raina plenty of time to play detec-tive with her grandma. By the end of it, Po Po would be back to harassing the high school kids to build her some new toys. And Raina could prove to Toni Moody that she was a competent apprentice. This couldn't work out any better.

"Are you staying the weekend?" She put on a forlorn frown but secretly hoped she had two days to herself.

"I'm not sure yet. I'll let you know," he said. "I guess it depends on whether or not your cousins have plans."

"What's the training for?"

"Administrative stuff like resource planning and budgeting for a small town police force. Helpful if I wanted to be chief someday."

"That's good, right?"

He gave her a sideways glance and nodded.

Raina dropped the subject. Obviously he didn't want to talk about it. Matthew was a man of action; a desk job—even for a promotion—would cage him in. It sure would be nice to be Mrs. Police Chief though.

She filled him in on what she discovered at the day spa. "Even if Po Po had filled the car with laughing gas, it wouldn't make sense. I know a kidnapping when I see one."

"Were the two of you smoking a joint?"

Raina narrowed her eyes at him. What was he implying? "No."

"I'm just checking. I heard a rumor that if someone couldn't get a prescription for medicinal use, Po Po could hook them up."

"My grandmother isn't a drug dealer."

"I didn't say she was selling it."

Raina blinked. What was her grandma doing in her spare time? Probably rumors from her grandma's nemesis. They cropped up like mushrooms when her grandma was into one of her more...creative moods.

"Back to the subject of the kidnapping," Raina said. "I don't like looking stupid in front of my new boss. Something is going on here, and I want to find out what it is."

"Oh, Rainy, let this go. You can impress Toni Moody by doing billable work."

"I wasn't planning to do it on company time. I work

twenty hours a week and have only one class left this semester. I still have plenty of time to ask a few questions."

"What about your thesis paper?"

"If it takes me an entire semester to write a paper, then I'm not fit for employment."

"What about me? Shouldn't we spend more time together?"

Raina gave him her best wide-eyed look. "Are you ready to set a date so we can start making arrangements?"

Matthew blinked, his face becoming unreadable. Raina chuckled at her ribbing. He wasn't ready and neither was she.

A Chinese wedding was a huge undertaking, best left until after her graduation. The guest list was already three hundred people long. After Po Po, Matthew's grandma, and her mom got their hands on the list, it would probably grow even longer. She suppressed a shiver.

Matthew chortled at the look on her face. "If that's what you want." He pulled her onto his lap and nibbled on her ear. "But I can think of a better use of our time at the moment."

Raina pushed him away reluctantly, inhaling his clean water and sage scent. Was the smell from his bath soap or his deodorant? "Stop it." It came out in a sigh. Not even remotely convincing to her own ears.

He moved from her ear to her lips, making her

forget all about Mia Westchester for the rest of the evening. Unfortunately he had already left the next morning when she got the call from her grandma.

3

DEAD WRONG

Raina woke to her cell phone chirping and vibrating on her nightstand. The other side of her queen bed was empty. Matthew had left at midnight because he had to drive to the Bay Area in the morning.

She glanced at the display on her phone. The call was from her grandma. Why would Po Po call at seven in the morning? "Morning," she mumbled into the phone.

"Rainy? Are you still in bed?" Po Po asked.

"It was a late night."

"What were you doing? Studying?"

"Um, sure." For someone who spoke a big game about bedroom gymnastics, her grandma wasn't nearly as experienced as she pretended to be. "Isn't it a little early for phone calls?"

"I found out something interesting about the

Westchesters. Want to have breakfast at the Pancake House?"

Arthur Westchester had fired Moody Investigation from the case. Even though Raina was curious about what happened to Mia Westchester, the smart thing to do was to let it go and get back in bed.

"Their seasonal pumpkin pancakes will be gone in another two weeks," Po Po said.

Raina yawned. Her grandmother could be like a terrier with a bone when she made up her mind. And nobody else made pumpkin chocolate chip pancakes like the Pancake House. "Give me thirty minutes. I'll pick you up."

She swung her legs out of bed and shuffled to the restroom to do her morning business. Matthew was right. This curiosity streak of hers would get her into trouble someday. Then it was a good thing she was engaged to a cop so he could bail her out, said a small voice in her head.

Forty minutes later she pulled up to the curb outside the front lobby of the senior condo complex. Her stomach was growling, but she ignored it. Another fifteen minutes or so and she would be stuffing her face with homemade pancakes topped with whipped cream. She would have to extend her evening run, but it was so worth it.

Through the glass lobby doors, she could see Po Po chatting with Frank Small, her grandma's newly promoted wingman now that her best friend had problems with her vision. Po Po waved goodbye to her friend and came out a moment later.

"Change of plans," Po Po said, buckling her seatbelt. "We need to get out to the old pumpkin patch on the south side of town."

"There are two in the area. Which pumpkin patch are you talking about?" Raina asked.

"The one the City Council wanted to develop into a mall."

Raina knew exactly which pumpkin patch her grandma was talking about now. The twenty-five acres were rezoned from agriculture to commercial a few years ago. There was a big stink at the time about money greasing politicians' hands according to her friend Eden, who was born and raised in Gold Springs. Nothing had come of it though, other than the large faded "Coming Soon" sign on the side of the road.

"I haven't had breakfast yet," Raina said as her stomach protested audibly again. "See? The beast wants food."

Po Po pulled a granola bar from her purse and shoved it toward Raina. "Here you go."

Raina sneered at the offering. Did her grandma think this poor substitute would compensate for freshly made pumpkin pancakes and hot coffee? "I don't think so. You said breakfast, and I want breakfast." All right, so she was starting to sound a bit whiny, but she wasn't skipping breakfast for a wild goose chase.

"Frank Small picked up a message from the police

scanner. A farmer heading into town found Arthur Westchester lying facedown in the dirt. He fell over a metal rake, and it killed him."

Raina's jaw dropped open. Someone kidnapped his wife yesterday, and he died today. He didn't strike her as someone particularly clumsy. This couldn't be an accident. "Are you sure?"

"Why do you think we're heading to the old pumpkin patch? It is not to look at the progress of the mall."

Raina straightened at a sudden thought. Was Arthur Westchester the developer for the contentious mall? He had to be. It was too much of a coincidence for his body to be found on the site otherwise.

"The Westchesters sound cursed," Po Po continued. "I hope they don't have kids, or they might be next."

"No kids, but there is an ex-wife. But from what I heard, it was an amicable divorce," Raina said absent-mindedly.

"No divorce is ever truly amicable. Someone is bound to have hurt feelings. They wouldn't have gotten married otherwise."

"I wonder who is out to get them," Raina said, thinking about her first interaction with the business tycoon.

Arthur Westchester had seemed like a kind man. Even though he exuded the kind of confidence that came from generations of power and wealth, he didn't seem to be the arrogant sort. But then again, what she knew about the hostile business world could fit into a postage stamp.

"What about the ex-wife? I bet you she has the most to gain from his death," Po Po said.

"Legalities from the first marriage were probably settled before the second marriage, so the first wife wouldn't get anything else from his death. It would be his second wife or business partner who would benefit from this."

"What does he do for a living again?" Po Po asked.

"He's a developer. He buys cheap land and turns it into a housing subdivision or commercial space."

"That sounds like a nifty job. How does one get a gig like this?"

Raina chuckled. "I have no idea. I'm sure he had old money in his family. They would be a privileged class, kind of like your family in China if your parents held onto the money."

Po Po sighed. "With this kind of money, there's plenty of reason for somebody to want him dead."

Raina gobbled the entire granola bar before she even made it down the street. At the first Starbucks, she pulled into the drive-thru despite the protest of her grandma and ordered a latte and a breakfast sandwich. By the time she hit the highway at the edge of town, she was feeling close to her normal self again. The pumpkin patch was off the first exit heading south.

"I'm supposed to turn off Lonesome Road, right?" Raina asked, squinting at the road signs.

"Yep," Po Po said.

The grove of trees in front of them cleared and the land became flat as far as the eye could see. Flashing lights clumped together like a herd of cows next to the field. Sirens approached them from behind, and Raina slowed the car and pulled over to the side of the two-lane road. A police cruiser rushed past.

Raina checked over her shoulder to make sure there were no more emergency vehicles and pulled back onto the road. She parked next to Eden Small's car, the local reporter and her former best friend. They'd had a falling out in the spring. Eden had tried to make small gestures of reconciliation, but Raina wasn't ready, and now she didn't have the time for it.

Raina and Po Po trotted up to the taped-off crime scene to stand next to the other lookie-loos. The body and rake were nowhere in sight, and the police appeared be interviewing the witness.

Her grandma drifted off to chat with a couple in overalls and work boots. Both of them had on wide-brimmed hats to protect their faces and gloves. But they didn't have the weathered appearance of someone who worked the land for a living. The coveralls were still too stiff with starch, and their faces were too pale, probably from sitting in an office job. They seemed like aged actors pretending to be farmers. She wondered who they were.

Raina strode over to her former BFF. "Hi."

Eden looked up from her notebook. Her deep brown face lit up into a smile that reached her soft brown eyes. "Rainy! What are you doing here?"

"Your grandfather heard the news through the police scanner at the senior center. And you know how he tells my grandmother everything." Raina shrugged. Once upon a time, she would have told Eden the details of the Westchester case, and they would have teamed up together.

"Let me guess—Po Po can't wait until tomorrow's edition of the *Gold Springs Weekly* to get the news?" Eden smiled good-naturedly. She had known Raina's grandma for some time.

"She didn't have to twist my arm too hard. I'm curious how someone could fall on a rake and kill himself. Did you find out anything?"

"Not much. The area around the body is muddy from last night's rain, so the possibility of slipping is plausible. Though no one knows why he was out here this early."

Raina frowned. Even if he'd had a business meeting with a surveyor or engineer, it would've been too dark to see the site. "What if somebody dumped his body out here?"

"You mean the whole thing could be a setup?"

"Well, the mall construction is not moving forward anytime soon now."

"The police wouldn't tell me anything. Maybe Matthew—"

"No."

"I'm not asking—"

"We don't talk about his work," Raina said, which wasn't strictly true, but no one needed to know this.

"We don't want to jeopardize his future opportunities with the department, so we don't talk about work."

Eden blew out a frustrated puff of air. "I can always ask Donna."

Given the right motivation, Donna, the desk clerk at the police station could be quite chatty. "She likes chocolate and cake," Raina said, ignoring her friend's grateful look. "Has anyone talked to Mia Westchester yet?"

Eden shook her head. "The body left for the morgue fifteen minutes ago. They probably have to do paperwork first. It might be another hour before they notify her."

An idea formed in Raina's head. Should she talk to the wife before the police get there? This was probably a stupid idea...and risky. Her pulse drummed with excitement. It would give her a chance to ask about the kidnapping. "Thanks for the info. I have to go get my grandmother before she breaks something or offends someone."

"Are you planning to investigate this murder?" Eden asked.

"I don't know what you're talking about," Raina said, averting her gaze.

"Sure, you don't. Just be careful. I heard his wife got kidnapped yesterday."

"Who did you hear this from?" Raina asked. *Please don't say Brenda Sullivan.* It was bad enough she couldn't discuss this case with her friends like she previously did, but to find out her one confidant was telling folks her secrets would be devastating.

"Detective Sokol came in to get coffee in the afternoon complaining about the wild goose chase. Speaking of the Venus Café..." Eden shuffled her feet, looking at the ground. "I found a full-time job in the mailroom for the *Sacramento Bee*. It's not ideal, but I could work my way up to being a reporter. It starts in two weeks." She looked at Raina. "I'm turning in my resignation at the café."

Raina studied her friend, pausing to consider her words. "I pulled in a favor to get you the job. You've been there for a few months." She didn't know what to say to Brenda Sullivan the next time she stopped by the Venus Café.

Eden studied the ground, shuffling her feet around the mud. "And thank you. That's why I'm telling you first before I say anything to Brenda."

"Are you moving to Sacramento?"

"I don't know yet. I guess it depends on the commute."

"What about Frank?"

"My grandfather will be fine. He'll have your grandmother to keep him company. He's always telling me to conquer the world. He's right. Other than a few day trips, I've spent my entire life in this town."

"Does this sudden move have anything to do with a new boyfriend?" Raina asked.

Eden had a habit of choosing losers for boyfriends so she could save them. Inevitably, she ended up holding the bag when they walked out on her or broke her heart. This trait had put a strain on their friendship more than once in the past.

"Nope, just a new opportunity," Eden said.

"I wish you the best of luck."

Raina started toward her grandma. She felt a small pang of regret. Eden had been her first friend when Raina had moved to Gold Springs a few years ago.

"Wait! Do you want to get together for lunch sometime?" Eden called out.

Raina turned around but kept walking backward. "Sure. I'll call you." While their friendship had run its course, it wouldn't hurt to say a final goodbye. She waved one last time to Eden and resumed trotting toward her grandma.

She pulled out her cell phone and texted Matthew, asking if he was staying in the Bay Area for the weekend. He replied with an affirmative. This meant he would be out of town for the next week and a half. Plenty of time for sleuthing with Po Po. If her grandma was already hinting about being left out now, how would she react when children came into the picture?

She waved to Po Po and the fake farmers. Upon closer inspection, her earlier assessment was dead on. No roughened skin or farmer's tan, although the husband looked as if he were recovering from a recent sunburn. And by the bright eyes and the curl at the corner of their lips, the neighbors didn't appear too upset with Arthur Westchester's death.

Raina signaled to Po Po again, trying to get her

grandma's attention. She slammed into someone and landed on the stem of a pumpkin. It jammed onto her backside. As she rolled over on the dirt, her left butt cheek cramped. She winced at the pain and lay there for a moment to catch her breath. Why did stuff like this always happen to her?

She glanced up at familiar blue eyes and a scowling baby doll face. Officer Hopper extended a hand, and Raina waved it aside. She couldn't have gotten up even if she wanted to. "I'm sorry I ran into you."

Officer Hopper dropped the hand. "What are you doing here at a crime scene?"

Raina batted her eyes, hoping she looked innocent. "Would you believe me if I said I was out for a morning stroll?"

Officer Hopper put a hand on her jutting hip, her expression stern. "Fool me again, and it'll be shame on me."

"The kidnapping wasn't a hoax. And now with her husband's death, it's obvious something is wrong in the Westchesters' household."

Officer Hopper kneeled next to Raina so they could be at the same eye level. "Matthew wouldn't want you sticking your nose in this business."

"I know, but he's not in town."

"This is no way to start a marriage."

Raina stiffened. She didn't need marriage advice from an ex-romantic rival even if she happened to be right. "Who made you the marriage expert?"

"I'm just saying."

"I don't hide anything from Matthew. He knows perfectly well I'm…" *Nosy and prideful?* These weren't traits Raina wanted to admit to herself, and especially not out loud to Joanna Hopper. "Professionally invested in this case."

"Just stay out of Detective Sokol's path. He's out to prove himself."

"What for?" Raina asked. The detective had once admitted to wanting Matthew's job. However, unless her fiancé got fired or promoted, there wasn't a vacancy.

Officer Hopper shrugged. "Don't know. Don't care."

"What about you? Don't you want to prove to the guys at the station you're just as good as them?"

"What do you think? I'm the only woman on the force, and only one step above the clerk."

"I think we should team up and solve this case before Detective Sokol does."

Officer Hopper narrowed her eyes and studied Raina for several long seconds, seeming to consider the offer. "No. I don't need Matthew upset with me if something happens to you. Just so we're clear—if he so much as offers me his pinkie, I'm taking it."

A weight settled on Raina's chest at the thought of Matthew leaving her. If things didn't work out, it wouldn't be over another woman. "Then I best practice on the fireman pole in my bedroom like my grandma suggested."

Officer Hopper rolled her eyes and stalked off, her blonde French braid swinging behind her.

Raina rubbed her butt cheek and slowly got up. Officer Hopper hadn't denied the suggestion of foul play. As a matter of fact, she had given away vital information—Arthur Westchester's death had to be murder.

4

THE BIG BAD WOLF

Raina hobbled the rest of the way to her grandma. It was probably her imagination, but it seemed as if everyone snickered behind their hands.

"Are you okay?" Po Po called out.

"Yep, just a bruised ego," Raina said.

The fake farmers took one look at Raina and melted away. She watched them go without a word. Sure, she was a klutz, but it wasn't catching. The couple seemed mighty unfriendly for folks in this area.

Raina tilted her head toward her car. "Let's roll." Once they hit the road, she asked her grandma, "Did you find out anything from the fake farmers?"

"Who?" Po Po asked.

"The neighbors."

"Why the nickname?"

Raina explained her observations. "A peeling sunburn a farmer does not make."

"You're partially right, Yoda. Their names are Aledo and Sandra Rankin. They retired last year, sold their house in Alameda, and moved here to live off the grid. They sunk all their money into the property so they could start a co-op. They're trying to convince their friends from the Bay Area to join them."

"They say anything about finding Arthur Westchester's body?"

Po Po shook her head. "Nothing more than what I heard on the police scanner. Aledo saw Arthur's truck on his private road, so he came over to check it out. He called out, but Arthur didn't answer. So Aledo walked over to the pumpkin patch and found the body."

"The pumpkin patch is a bit of a walk from the road. Why would Aledo do this?"

Po Po shrugged. "Beats me. Why would anybody want to live off the grid? I don't understand crazy people."

Raina gave Po Po a sideways glance and returned her gaze to the road. Some people would say the same thing about her grandma. "It would give me a mild heart attack to find a body in my backyard, but he doesn't seem rattled by it."

"He's a former FBI agent. Maybe he's used to seeing bodies."

"I wonder if he wants to be a volunteer deputy."

"I can feel a great disturbance in your loyalty. It's shifting over to the police department."

"When is keeping our town safe a loyalty problem?"

"If I need to hide in your closet, you got my back, right? I don't need excuses on why I can't come in."

Raina nodded. What else could she say? "If it makes you feel any better, I'll clean out Matthew's half of the closet for you." Her grandma beamed at the suggestion. "Did you find out anything else about the Rankins?"

"No, nothing else about the death. They seem interested in how this will impact the mall project."

"Well, if the mall got built, the developer would bring the utilities and public infrastructure to their property line. Their land value would go up significantly, especially in the next housing boom. I'm not sure what will happen to the project now."

Po Po squinted at Raina, doubt written across her face. "Let me guess. This is the engineering degree I paid for."

Raina flushed. Was this a reprimand for not using her degree? She dismissed the thought. Her grandma didn't play mental games like her mother did. "We should visit Mia Westchester before the police get there."

"Do I sense trouble in paradise? Does he think he's the better detective again?"

Raina didn't like the knowing tone in her grandma's voice. "We're amateur hour compared to an experienced detective like Matthew." She put a slight emphasis on the word "experienced." "He's out of town, so he's not on the case."

Po Po did a fist pump and whooped. "Looks like it's just you and me, kid. We'll show them how it's done."

Raina grimaced. While she appreciated her grandma's confidence, they were nothing more than nosy looky-loos to the police. "That's not technically correct. Officer Hopper mentioned that Detective Sokol would be on the case. They must suspect homicide too."

"How is Arthur's death connected to the kidnapping yesterday?"

"No idea. But let's see what Mia Westchester has to say about it." Raina paused as her thoughts took a tangent. "Does this make us ambulance chasers?"

"Nope, we have no financial gain for helping out. Besides, Mia doesn't know about the death yet, so this will be a friendly chat."

Raina bit her lower lip, considering her grandma's words. She wouldn't call this visit a friendly chat, but it was probably a matter of perspective. "My boss wouldn't like me looking into this."

"Toni Moody has to know it would be her loss if she ends the internship," Po Po said. "You have to fill this niche when she retires in a few years. Folks shouldn't have to drive to Sacramento for a PI to take care of private matters."

Raina doubted the pragmatic Toni would care where folks drove to take care of their business. Matthew might be right. If she wanted to impress her new boss, she would be better off drumming up new business for Moody Investigation. But she couldn't get into private investigation thinking of her bank account statement, or it would become just another job.

As Raina rolled back into town, they were silent for several minutes. She weaved her way to the expensive neighborhood she didn't know existed until Arthur Westchester walked into the Moody Investigation office. Unlike the previous deaths she had encountered, this one didn't leave her with an overwhelming sense of sadness.

"Investigating Arthur Westchester's death has nothing to do with Matthew or Toni. I need to know this desire to be a private investigator isn't a fluke. What if this turns out to be like my engineering career? I can't afford to keep reinventing myself."

Po Po groaned, covering her face with her hands. "Why do young people make things so complicated? You don't have to figure out your life's purpose every time you pick your belly button lint. Just find a passion and pursue it with reckless abandon. When that runs out, find another passion. How hard is that?"

Raina pulled up next to the curb outside the Westchester McMansion. "I can't afford to keep pursuing passions. I'm about to graduate with a master's degree in a couple of months that qualifies me for a secretarial job if I'm lucky."

"Ah-ha! I knew it. It's your father talking here. He was another one of those engineers who could only think inside his box." Po Po held up her fingers, ticking off the points. "You're young, and you have an inheritance and a safety net"—she pointed at herself. "Have fun, Rainy. You'll never have this time again."

They got out of the car in silence. Raina knew her grandma was right, but she was tired of being the loser in her extended family. At least she was engaged and no longer "on the shelf." This ought to count for something at the next family reunion. It still rankled though, being judged on the letters after her name.

Raina's cell phone chirped at an incoming text. She pulled it out from her purse and checked the message. Her jaw dropped.

"Who is it from? And what does it say?" Po Po asked, trying to peer at the screen.

"It's Cassie, and she's dropping Lila off. Apparently, she and my brother-in-law decided they need a getaway at Lake Tahoe."

Po Po broke into a broad smile. "All right. We get the baby girl all to ourselves."

"I'm glad you're excited about potty training the child all weekend because I'm not."

"The nanny isn't coming?"

Raina shook her head and felt a flash of satisfaction when the smile slipped off her grandma's face. Like her sister, her grandma had only changed diapers a handful of times even though she had seven children. Raina did a little jig on the sidewalk and sang, "There's something strange in the dirty diaper. Who are you gonna call? Po Po. It's kinda green and a little lumpy—"

Po Po pulled out the homemade pumpkin launcher from her purse. "Do you want to continue this?"

Raina held up both hands. "All right. I'll stop."

"So what's the game plan?" Po Po said, tucking the pumpkin launcher back into her backpack.

Raina rang the doorbell. "We're concerned citizens who witnessed the kidnapping. We'll wing it from there."

A dog started barking inside the house. The last time Raina encountered a little lap dog, he took an instant disliking to her and yapped within sniffing distance of her. She hoped it wouldn't be the case this time.

The door cracked open, and Mia Westchester peeked out. A black Labrador retriever that was the size of a small bear launched forward—snapping its big teeth inches from Po Po's face—and hit the doorframe. Her grandma screamed, frozen to the spot.

Raina jerked the door closed, holding onto the knob. The door jumped in her hands from the force of a body slamming into it.

Bam! Bam!

"Poe! No!" Mia's voice could be heard through the closed door. "Consuela! Take Poe to the backyard, *por favor.*"

There was a faint shuffling noise, and then it was quiet on the other side. The front door opened again, and Mia came out. "Sorry about that. I don't know what spooked Poe. He's normally such a sweet dog."

Raina gave her a doubtful look. The big bad wolf

probably seemed like a sweet animal before he took out Red Riding Hood's granny. She grabbed onto her grandma's arm. "Your dog almost gave my grandma a heart attack."

Po Po took the hint, clutching at her chest and rolling her eyes back. "My heart! It hurts."

Mia glanced at the elderly woman with wide eyes. "Oh my gosh! Should I call nine-one-one?"

Raina tried not to wince at the overdone theatrics. "No, I think she'll be fine in a few minutes. Can we come inside, so she doesn't have to stand in the sun?"

Mia held open the door. "Of course! There's a chair by the stairs."

Raina averted her face so Mia couldn't see the smile threatening to peek out.

The foyer was the size of her apartment with a tile mosaic medallion underneath the crystal chandelier. The purple velvet drapes next to the front door were shredded into ribbons. The side table tipped onto its side. It looked like somebody had been on a rampage.

Raina crossed the foyer, holding onto her grandma's arm. Po Po shuffled and clutched at her heart, moaning every few steps. If Raina hadn't known her grandma didn't have a heart condition, she would be worried. Po Po sank onto the chair with a heavy sigh.

Mia hovered anxiously next to them, wringing her hands. "Does she need water or anything?"

"I'm all right, my dear. I just need a minute," Po Po croaked, pulling out a tissue to blot at her dry face. "Why don't the two of you chat while I recover?"

Raina bit her lower lip to keep from giggling. Her grandma fell into her role like she had been practicing all morning. "You don't know me, but I used to work at the day spa."

"Yes, the front desk girl with the weather name." Mia glanced at Raina's curly hair. "Not too many Chinese girls with hair like yours either."

Raina grimaced. She was notorious for her rat nest hair. Fabulous. At least she was memorable. "I'm Raina Sun." She gestured at Po Po. "And this is my grandmother, Bonnie Wong. Yesterday we were at the corner of Broadstone and Lafayette when we saw..." She pretended to hesitate.

"Two men stuffing you into a van," Po Po cut in, forgetting her heart condition. "It looked like you got kidnapped."

"Ummm...that can't be me," Mia said, gesturing at herself. "As you can see, I'm here. My husband wouldn't be able to get the ransom money this quickly." She smiled at her joke, but her gaze shifted across them, making no eye contact.

"It was you, all right," Po Po said. "There's not too many women with your va-va-voom curves." She made the gesture of an hourglass with her hands. "Must be the hot Latin blood."

Raina bit the inside of her cheek to stop herself from laughing. Her grandma had been a proper Chinese wife in public most of her adult life. But after her husband's death, she decided the charade had gone on long enough. These days, no one could predict what came out of her grandma's mouth.

"We need some of that blood in our family. We're all thin as a rail and flat as—"

"Po Po! Behave!" Raina cut her grandma off, not because she didn't want to hear the rest of her thoughts, but because Mia was starting to get the caged look.

"Thank you?" Mia glanced around as if looking for an excuse for them to leave. "Are you feeling better already? I have to go. My dog needs his medication."

"It looks like your dog might need Prozac," Po Po said, gesturing at the shredded curtains.

Mia's lips thinned into a tight smile. "You need to go now."

"Wait!" Raina called out. Since Arthur Westchester was dead, client confidentiality wasn't an issue anymore. "Your husband hired us to spy on you while he's at work. That's how we ended up witnessing the kidnapping."

"Hired the two of you?" Mia asked, her voice full of incredulity. Her eyes darted between Raina and her grandma.

Po Po puffed out her chest like a rooster in a hen yard. "That's because we're super spies."

Mia burst out laughing. "I don't have time for this."

Po Po crossed her arms and gripped the seat of the chair. "You'll have to drag me out screaming."

Mia raised an eyebrow. "Consuela! My shot gun, *por favor*," she called out.

Raina grabbed her grandma's arm and hauled her up.

"Coming, Mum," a voice called out. Footsteps sounded in the hallway, followed by a banging cabinet.

"We should probably get going," Raina said, dragging her grandma across the foyer. A bead of sweat rolled down the small of her back. She had no idea whether or not Mia was bluffing, but she wasn't taking her chances, especially with her grandma in the room.

Mia stalked a step behind them, her expression unreadable. Gone was the concerned woman they had seen earlier.

"Why did your husband go to the old pumpkin patch this morning?" Raina called out over her shoulder. She opened the door and pushed her grandma through first in case Mia started shooting.

"Mum, here's your gun," a voice called out from the foyer.

Raina turned around in time for the door to slam shut and the lock to slide home. The tension between her shoulder blades eased. This was too close for comfort.

Po Po pounded on the door. "Hey! What happened to old-fashioned hospitality? I could use a glass of iced tea."

The dog barked from the other side of the door.

Bam! Bam!

The door rattled in front of them.

Raina jumped at the noise. "What the—"

"She's going to let the dog loose," Po Po said.

They backed away from the door and trotted to the faded red Honda parked on the curb. In this neighborhood, the car squatted next to the curb like a bag lady. Across the street, a police cruiser pulled up, and Officer Hopper got out. Another door slammed, and the top half of Detective Youri Sokol's head appeared across the roof of the vehicle. Wonderful. Her favorite duo.

5

CALL ME MAYBE

As the two cops crossed the street, Raina couldn't help but notice the contrast between the two. Detective Sokol reached Officer Hopper's chin but carried himself like he was a much taller man. He had the handsome good looks of a younger Danny DeVito, if one liked the loose jowls and pug nose. Instead of scowling at Raina like Officer Hopper was doing, he gave her a broad smile like he was greeting an old friend. Yikes! He was up to no good, and he probably thought Raina could help him.

Even if Mia had called the police on them, they couldn't have gotten here this quickly. This meant they were here to deliver the bad news to the widow. Time to hightail it out of here before things got ugly.

Officer Hopper stalked over and invaded Raina's personal space, towering over her. "What are you doing here? You didn't tell Mia Westchester about..." Her voice trailed off.

Raina recoiled. "No! That's your job to deliver the news." She was offended at Officer Hopper's tone. "I might be nosy, but I'm not insensitive. I came to ask her about the kidnapping."

Officer Hopper narrowed her eyes. "And?"

"She denies it ever happened."

"She was at the day spa." Officer Hopper spat out each word like they were bullets. "You wasted my entire morning. The town should bill you for the stupid prank."

Raina winced. Somebody was having a bad day. She wondered if Detective Sokol had anything to do with the change in Officer Hopper's mood from an hour earlier.

"I was there," Po Po said. "I witnessed—"

"The town's drug supplier for the geriatric crowd isn't the most reliable witness...or most upstanding citizen," Officer Hopper said.

"Now wait one minute—"

A loud piercing whistle cut through the air. The dog inside the house went wild, howling like it was the full moon. Even from the sidewalk, Raina could hear the door rattling as if the dog was slamming into it with his body. She clapped her hands over her ears.

Detective Sokol lowered his fingers from his mouth. "Ladies, please don't make me do this again."

Officer Hopper rolled her eyes and headed up the driveway. "Just stay out of my way, Raina."

The detective waited until his partner was halfway

up the driveway before he held out a business card. "Call me. Let's have coffee sometime."

Raina's eyes widened. Why? He was married, and she was not interested.

He must have read her thoughts. Because he added, "I want to talk about the Westchester case."

"I don't work for the police department."

"But your fiancé does. And this makes us almost family."

As she watched the detective catch up to his partner, she frowned. The fraternity was strong at the police department, but Detective Sokol was not family. Raina understood his drive for advancement since he was the sole breadwinner and father to new twin boys.

However, he would undoubtedly take any information or insight from Raina and present it as his own. She didn't care, except now she had to think of Matthew. Detective Sokol would be his primary competitor for the promotion.

"What a weasel," Po Po mumbled, opening the door to Raina's car.

There wasn't much Raina could say to defend the man. She pulled away from the curb and drove toward the Venus Café. The mom-and-pop shops in the historic downtown were getting ready for the lunch rush with clapboard signs announcing specials or sales. She stopped for a bicyclist and parked.

Raina held open the door to the café. "We should patronize another restaurant sometimes. We were here yesterday."

Po Po stepped through. "Why? The food is good, and the price is right."

"Right now I crave a fresh out-of-the-oven dan tat." Raina's mouth salivated at the thought of biting into the crispy shell of a creamy egg tart. Living in a small town didn't offer much in culinary delights.

"Too bad the nearest Chinese bakery is in Sacramento. We should open a small Chinese bakery. If you run it, I'm sure we could make a profit."

Raina wrinkled her nose. The hours would be long, and profits would be slim, especially if her grandma gave away half their stock to her cronies. Within weeks of opening, the bakery would become a senior citizen hang out. "Now that would be cliché. A baking amateur sleuth. No, thanks."

"I'm just giving you options since you're having a conniption about finding a passion."

"You sound more worried about this passion than me." It was sweet for her grandma to be so concerned, but Raina didn't need the pressure.

They placed their order at the counter, grabbed their drinks, and settled at a table. Brenda had replaced the red-and-white-checkered vinyl tablecloths with orange-and-black ones. On the center of each table was a small bowl of candy.

Po Po unwrapped a Tootsie roll and popped it into her mouth. "With Matthew out of town, I'm worried Detective Sokol's incompetence will compromise the case. The bad guys should behave when Matthew is away."

Raina snorted. "Hold on. Let me call the bad guys to let them know this is the new plan."

Po Po gave Raina the stink eye. "Stop being so hangry."

"Being hungry has nothing to do with my crankiness level. I'm just tired of budget cuts that keep reducing the police force." Raina blew out a puff of air, hoping it would reduce her crankiness. She was getting hangry. "If I tell Matthew about the murder investigation, he would be back by tomorrow."

"Don't you dare! He needs the training to be chief."

"But he doesn't want a promo—"

"The training would give him options and a leg up if he were to compete with Detective Sokol in an interview."

Raina knew her grandma was right, but this meant they would have to put up with Detective Sokol fumbling through the case. "While I am willing to help the police, I'm not sure Toni Moody would be as understanding if it took up too much of my time. I don't want to lose this opportunity with her."

Po Po waved dismissively. "If you're meant to be a PI, the universe will find a way for you to be one. Don't worry. I'll say an extra prayer to our ancestors for you."

Brenda showed up with their lunch, saving Raina from answering her grandma. She didn't think an extra prayer would help, but someone up there had to be looking out for her. Things had turned out okay so far even with the bumblings and misunderstandings in her life.

"Have you seen Eden lately?" Brenda asked. "She hasn't shown up for work in two days."

Raina averted her gaze, glancing at the Cobb salad in front of her. Great. Her former friend probably didn't care to call in anymore with a new job waiting in the wings. Should she tell Brenda what Eden had told her? She was never recommending someone for a job again.

Po Po reached for the ketchup bottle and drowned her fries in the red goo. "She was at the old pumpkin patch this morning."

"I see," Brenda said, frowning. "Is she reporting on the murder then?"

Raina's eyes widened. The coroner couldn't have finished the autopsy report this quickly. "How do you know it's murder?"

Brenda shrugged, leaving extra napkins next to Po Po's plate. "What else can it be? Arthur Westchester is not the type of man to wake up with the barn rooster. He usually stumbles in at ten for his first cup of coffee."

"I thought a businessman was supposed to be an early to bed, early to rise type," Po Po said.

"Not Arthur. Sometimes he swung by to pick up his dinner at eight. If he was eating that late, I doubt he was going to bed at nine," Brenda said.

"But who told you about Arthur's death in the first place? It's not public information yet," Raina said.

Brenda glanced around, dropping her voice to a

whisper. "Peaches La Farge told me about it when she delivered her pies—"

Po Po's eyes widened. "You serve Peaches' Pies—"

"Shhh!" Brenda hushed her. "I'm not a baker. And her prices are reasonable."

"How does Peaches know about his death?" Raina asked, steering the conversation back on topic.

"She lives on the other side of the grove," Brenda said. "You can't see her house from the private road." A customer came in, and Brenda returned to the cash register to help him.

Raina and Po Po spent the next ten minutes inhaling their food. The cheeseburger didn't have a fighting chance with her grandma. Raina regretted the salad after the first bite. She would grow tired of the chewing before her hunger would be satisfied.

"Why was Arthur at the old pumpkin patch so early in the morning?" Po Po said, blotting her mouth with a napkin.

Raina finished chewing and swallowed. "Either his body was dumped at the site, or he was lured out there. Under both scenarios, the killer would have contacted Arthur to make arrangements for a meeting. Mia Westchester should know whether her husband's behavior changed recently or if someone called him last night."

"How can we get her to talk? Her beast of a dog and shotgun are more than enough to keep me away."

"Maybe we can approach her from a different angle. If only we knew who her kidnappers were."

"I can take care of that," Po Po said, tapping her chest. "One of my high schoolers is a talented artist. She can sketch out a picture for us, and we can plaster his mug all over town. Someone is bound to know the guy. And if not, seeing the picture might be enough to get Mia talking."

Raina considered her grandma's plan. It was a good one, but... "Please don't post your phone number on the flyer. I don't want the kidnapper luring you to a dark alley."

"Or another pumpkin patch. Don't worry. I'll get one of those prepaid phones. You can even keep it to take the call. It's not like you couldn't use a spare phone."

Raina ignored the last comment. It wasn't her fault she had bad juju when it came to cell phones. "I should meet with Detective Sokol to see what he wants."

"We already know what he wants. The weasel man wants you to solve the case for him, tie it in a pretty bow, and let him take the credit for it. He probably thinks he'll get a promotion out of this with Matthew out of the picture."

"But he could let us know what is in the autopsy report."

Po Po snorted. "Arthur impaled himself on a rake at dawn. There'll be nothing in the autopsy report to say it was an accident. What other possible information do we need?"

Raina knew her grandma was probably right.

"There's no harm in seeing what Detective Sokol has to say."

"Fine. You meet with him then. I'm not wasting my time. I have to talk to the insurance agent and meet with the high schoolers this afternoon."

Raina frowned at her grandma. "Why are you meeting with the high school kids?"

Po Po widened her eyes. "I'm mentoring them."

"Uh-huh. If you end up in jail, I'm not bailing you out."

"Urgh! You make it sound like I'm up to no good." Po Po smirked, pleased with herself.

Raina suppressed a smile. Her grandma probably wanted the kids to develop a new toy for her. She didn't want to deal with Detective Sokol by herself. Her grandma had a way of keeping him off-balance, which might help with keeping him honest.

In the meantime, she could check out Arthur's business. Maybe someone in the office might have a clue on why someone would want to kill the boss.

"Arthur Westchester still has an outstanding bill with Moody Investigation for the last two days of surveillance work," Raina said. "I'll ask Toni if she wants me to drop off the bill at Westchester Development."

"Good thinking. Maybe you can find out something from the office manager."

"My thoughts exactly, but I'll keep this part of my task quiet for now."

"Afraid your boss would tell you to leave the case alone?"

"Maybe, but it's easier to ask for forgiveness later. Besides, I'm being proactive for collecting on an outstanding bill."

Raina ignored the churning in her stomach. She hadn't worked long enough with Toni Moody yet to know how her boss would react. However, time was of the essence. Once news of Arthur's death became public knowledge, everyone would clam up. After all, what healthy middle-aged man died from a fall on a farming rake at dawn?

6

ALL IN THE FAMILY

After dropping her grandma off at the senior condo complex, Raina drove to Moody Investigation. The office was empty. Toni must be still at lunch or running errands.

She opened the drawer containing their recent cases. She pulled out the Westchester file and flipped through the handwritten notes from Toni and herself. It was just as she remembered it.

There was no mention of the feud with the neighbors. Their investigation and surveillance of Mia Westchester probably had nothing to do with Arthur's death. Case closed for a practical businesswoman like Toni Moody. If they were to continue to investigate, there wouldn't be anyone to pay the bill.

Raina grabbed the outstanding invoice for Arthur Westchester from the file cabinet, pausing as her gaze dropped on Peaches La Fargo's folder on the desk.

Maybe the pie lady would know the gossip about the feud between Westchester Development and the Rankins.

She tucked both files into her purse and scribbled a note saying she would collect on both invoices for her boss. She left the office, glad she didn't have to talk to Toni in person. The longer she could delay their conversation, the better.

Her cell phone chirped from an incoming text message. It was from her sister.

BE THERE IN 30 MINUTES.

Raina grumbled under her breath, locking the office door on her way out. There went her afternoon plans. Maybe this was for the best. After all, Arthur's death would be public knowledge by tomorrow, and people's tongues might wag in the aftermath of the shocking news.

RAINA STOPPED by her apartment to grabbed the frozen dumplings from her freezer and headed to her grandma's condo. It had been a long day, and now it would be a much longer evening. When she walked in, the two-bedroom unit was lemon fresh and sparkling clean.

Unlike her house in San Francisco, her grandma's

condo was modern with tasteful furniture from Scandinavian Designs and bold decorations. Scattered throughout the unit were recent family photos. This home was a truer reflection of her grandma's soul than the antique furniture and fussy curtains in her Victorian.

"I guess the regular maid service wasn't up to snuff, huh?" Raina asked, heading straight for the kitchen. She pulled out a pot, filled it with water, and set it on the stove.

"What makes you think I didn't clean it myself?" Po Po said.

Raina raised an eyebrow. Uh-huh. Did her grandma think she was fooling anyone? "How did the meeting with the insurance agent go?"

"I'll probably need someone from Sacramento. The agent was pushing a burial service insurance. What do I need burial service for?" Po Po said, grabbing a brochure from the counter and handing it to Raina. "I have my family to *jup gwat*."

Raina glanced at the colorful brochure advertising customizable final arrangements. While her grandma might have her family to "pick up her bones" as the Chinese saying went, not all elderly people could count on the same luxury with their families. "I can see how this could be popular with the folks at the senior center."

"It's a white glove service for five thousand dollars. From the mortuary to the ground." Po Po shoved the brochure into her junk drawer. "I don't want to talk about this anymore. It's depressing."

Raina hugged her grandma. "Don't worry, Po Po. I'll make sure everyone is stinking drunk, so nobody will notice you're still in the attic of your house in San Francisco. That can be your final resting place."

Po Po snickered. "Your mom will love the smell."

Her grandma would have the grandest Chinese funeral available, not because she had money to burn, but because she liked the theatrics even at the end.

Raina suppressed a smile and opened the refrigerator. The carton of expired milk looked rather lonely next to the hunk of cheese with some white fuzz on it. "What are you planning to feed Lila?"

Her grandma had employed a cook when she lived in San Francisco. Since her move to Gold Springs, Raina had often filled in the role in exchange for groceries.

Po Po flushed. "Why do you think you're here? You're both the nanny and cook."

"I'm not sure if I should be flattered or offended."

"You can't tally this kind of stuff in our relationship, hon. It'll all even out in the end."

Raina glanced at the time displayed on the microwave. "I'll do a quick grocery run after we feed The Little Tornado. You can handle bath time on your own while I am out, right?"

Po Po tipped her chin up. "Now I'm not sure if I should be offended. I raised seven children—"

"With a nanny's help—"

"Not at first. I didn't have help until Ah Gong's business took off—"

Knock! Knock!

Po Po cut off her explanation and gave Raina the double thumbs up sign. "The Little Tornado is here. Just think of this as practice for when you have kids of your own with Matthew."

Raina followed her grandmother to the front door. It wasn't for her benefit she was here this weekend. The last time her grandma had spent more than a few hours caring for a child was over fifty years ago. Even though her grandma had kept in shape, it still took Raina a healthy dose of coffee to keep up with her three-year-old niece.

Po Po opened the front door. Cassie held Lila on one hip with a diaper bag slung over the other shoulder.

Her husband, Benson, held a stroller and a car seat. He handed over the equipment to Raina and said, "I'll get the rest of the stuff from the car."

Raina glanced at her older sister. There was more? "It's just for the weekend, right?"

Cassie smiled. "It's just her clothes, bath stuff, potty, and some toys. Please try to keep up with the potty training while she's here. We wouldn't want her to go backward."

Po Po held out her hand, drool practically dripping from her smile. "Come to Tai Po, Lila."

The toddler reached for her great-grandma. "TV in car, Tai Po."

"Is that right, honey," Po Po said, bouncing the child in her arms, and strode off toward the master bedroom suite.

"How was the drive up here?" Raina asked, setting down the car seat and stroller in front of the coat closet.

"It was okay. Lila watched a movie the entire way, so we didn't have to stop," Cassie said, pacing the length of the small living room.

Raina watched her sister stretch her legs. Cassie had dark eye bags like she hadn't slept for days. Her thick black hair had lost the sheen Raina had always envied. Today, her curly mop looked magazine perfect next to her sister.

With a full-time nanny and weekly maid service, Cassie shouldn't have the careworn look of some moms. Raina didn't know what was going on, but her grandma was right. Her sister was screaming for help. And there wasn't time for girl talk before she had to leave.

"Are you excited about getting some grown-up time this weekend?" Raina asked.

Cassie tried to smile, but it wobbled. Footsteps approached the condo, and Benson appeared with a small suitcase and a backpack.

He left it next to the stroller. "So are we sneaking out or saying goodbye?"

"Let me talk to her first," Cassie said. She disappeared into the bedroom.

Once her sister was out of earshot, Raina whispered, "Is everything okay? My sister isn't sick, is she?" Raina didn't believe her sister had health issues, but she couldn't ask if their marriage was okay.

Benson was an up-and-coming lawyer in her uncle's law firm and had always looked a little too suave for Raina's taste. But like Cassie, he didn't look his usual self today either. First, he had bed head. The front stuck out like a duck's tail, and the back was flattened like he had helmet hair. His shirt was still starched and stiff, but the back wasn't tucked in. He had never looked quite this relaxed in all the years Raina had known him.

"Life is good," Benson said. "One of the partners is talking about retiring next year. I think your uncle is grooming me to fill the spot."

"That's great," Raina said, trying to inject some enthusiasm into her voice.

His statement confirmed what Raina always suspected—he would never cheat on her sister because he was more interested in his career than other women. According to her grandma, a workaholic was better than a womanizer. Raina wasn't so sure. Either way, there was another mistress in his life.

He glanced at the master bedroom. "Your sister isn't happy with it though. She's probably getting bored and wants me home more. I better go say goodbye to the munchkin."

Cassie came out just as he was heading in. She edged around him so that he wouldn't brush her. She blinked at the tears in her eyes. "Take care of my baby for me, Rainy. This is the first time I've left her behind."

Raina rubbed her sister's back. "She'll be okay. Have fun on your weekend getaway."

"It's not a vacation. Our marriage counselor is hosting a weekend retreat at Lake Tahoe," Cassie said.

Raina's eyes widened. Marriage counseling? Maybe she should have paid more attention when her sister had complained about her marriage all summer. She opened her mouth, but Benson came back into the living room.

He paused, and his eyes shifted between the two women. "Girl talk? Do you want me to wait in the bedroom?" He jerked his thumb back at the direction he came from.

Cassie shook her head. "I was just telling Raina to take care of the baby. Let's go. The longer I stay, the more I think this is a bad idea."

Benson held out his hand. "Come, my lovely. Your carriage awaits."

Cassie took her husband's hand, and the couple left the condo.

Raina returned to the kitchen to resume dinner preparations. There was no point in joining her grandma until after she got her fill of Lila. Po Po didn't like to share until she ran out of steam.

As she put a pan on the stove for the frozen dumplings, her thoughts drifted back to her sister's marital issues. Was there trouble in paradise, or was her brother-in-law correct that her sister was a bored housewife? She wasn't sure her perfect older sister could handle being the first divorcee in their family. She prayed this was nothing more than a small speed bump in their marriage. She had to believe there were happily ever afters for the women in her family.

AFTER TUCKING in the twin toddlers, aka Lila and Po Po, Raina returned to her apartment to shower. In clean pajamas and feeling human again, she settled into her second-hand sofa to call Matthew to discuss her sister's marital problem.

"Just stay out of it, Rainy. They'll either work it out or they won't. Neither of them would appreciate you butting in. Besides, you'll want to keep things cordial with Benson for your niece's sake." Matthew's tone sounded slightly distracted.

Raina frowned at the phone. Didn't he know it was part of the sister code to be in each other's business? As an only child, of course, he didn't understand. She should discuss this with her grandma in the morning instead. "How is the training class—"

"How come you didn't tell me there was another murder in town?" Matthew asked.

Raina sat back into her sofa and suppressed a sigh. So he had heard about Arthur Westchester's death and waited for her to say something. How long had he known? She could already predict where this conversation would go. Once again it would probably start and end with butting out where she wasn't wanted.

This was the one aspect of their relationship that bugged her. It was all right for him to risk his life for justice, but not her. It shouldn't matter he was paid for the work. And it wasn't like she wouldn't be a peer of sorts when she got her private investigator license.

"...counting on you to keep an eye on things," Matthew said.

"Whoa! What?" Raina asked, her mind trying to catch up with his words. Did he just ask her to keep an eye on things at the police station? No way!

"I'm sorry, Rainy. But you're part of the family now. Joanna is dealing with a personal issue, and Youri is a loose cannon. I could call the dog catcher, but he's half-baked. So you'll have to keep an eye on things to make sure the investigation doesn't get compromised."

"Uh..." She should play it cool, sounding reluctant somehow. She didn't want him to think she was already up to her neck in the case.

"I'll try to get back as soon as I can. Maybe I can talk the chief into letting me leave early," he said, the words rushing out. "Just keep Youri from messing something up."

"Okay, but you owe me," Raina said, glad he couldn't see the smile on her face.

After they hung up, she texted Detective Sokol. He replied immediately with a time and address. So the next morning, she would have enough time to visit the pie lady and feed the kids, aka Po Po and Lila, stop by

Westchester Development, and meet with Detective Sokol. She was already tired thinking of all the driving about she would have to do. She prayed their ancestors were looking out for her sister because she certainly didn't have the time to help.

7

THE BOTTOM OF A PIE

The next morning, after feeding Po Po and Lila breakfast, Raina drove the three of them toward La Fargo farm to drop off the final report for the pie recipe theft case. Her grandma tapped away on her smarty-pants phone in the passenger seat, while her great-granddaughter tapped on her tablet in the car seat. It was uncanny how similar the two of them acted at times.

It was an uneventful drive. Just like her friend Brenda said, Raina couldn't see the old pumpkin patch from this side of the grove. The house came into view at the end of the long driveway.

Raina squinted, questioning what she saw. "Is that a miniature...French château?"

Po Po glanced up from her screen. "Man, we're in the wrong business. When did pies become so lucrative?"

"Pies yummy," Lila added from the back.

After Raina parked on the asphalt driveway, she slung the child on one hip and grabbed the report. When Raina pressed the doorbell, a little lilting harp music filled the air. Her niece clapped her hands and grinned with delight. Raina hoped there was no giant dog on the other side like at the Westchester's house.

A man in his fifties cracked open the door, holding it close so they couldn't see inside. "Yes?"

"Hi, I'm Raina Sun. I work for Moody Investigation, and I'm here to drop off the final report for the pie recipe thief."

The man gave her a squinty stare and jerked his chin at Po Po and Lila. "Who are they?"

"We're her entourage," Po Po said.

The man shifted his eyes back to Raina, curling one corner of his mouth. "Well, I'll be." He turned and hollered over his shoulder. "Peaches! That PI you hired is here." He came out and addressed Lila. "Do you like puppies? We have a new litter in the barn."

Lila clapped excitedly, bouncing against Raina's hip. "Doggy! Lila likes puppy. Go New Rain."

Raina's Chinese name written in the traditional style of surname first literally translated as *new rain*. Her niece had never called her anything else.

Po Po held out her hands. "I'll take the babe, Rainy."

Raina watched the three of them happily trot off for a building peeping out from the side of the Château de Pie. The door clicked open again, and

Raina turned back to the front door with a smile on her face.

Peaches La Fargo looked just like a pie tycoon should—sparkling blue eyes that crinkled at the corners and dimples like someone had pressed their thumbs on her cheeks. She was a couple of inches taller than Raina and several pounds heavier. Her dark brown hair with golden highlights fell in loose waves down her back.

Raina could tell her default expression was good humored, but at the moment, she looked nervous like she wasn't sure she wanted to hear the truth.

Peaches rubbed the back of her neck. "What did you find? Did the Rankins steal my pie recipes? I had never met less friendly people in my life. It's what happens when city folks decide they want to be farmers."

Raina knew she shouldn't be encouraging this gossip, but the pie lady could offer a new perspective on the case. "I heard that they were real upset about the mall Arthur Westchester wanted to build next-door."

"None of us want the mall here. It would ruin the rural feel of this area. I even offered to buy the property from Arthur so I can keep it undeveloped."

Raina pretended to gasp, opening her eyes wide. "You didn't...you didn't have anything to do with Arthur Westchester's death?" She was proud of the slight tremor in her voice. "Did you knock him out with a rolling pin before stabbing him with the rake?"

The pie lady snorted, rolling her eyes. "Honey, you're not that good of an actress. Why don't you just come out and ask me what you want to know?"

Raina flushed, slightly embarrassed. "I'm curious who would want to kill Arthur? He seemed like a nice man."

"Well, the couple from the Bay Area had a huge blowup fight with him about the access easement on their property. Apparently, Arthur and his lawyers interpreted the easement to mean the Rankins' private road could be an access road to the mall."

"Can the Rankins challenge the easement?"

"It was on the deed when they bought the property. If they didn't want people on their private road, they should have bought something else."

While this was true, Raina knew most people didn't read all the fine print when they were signing paper-work. "So you witnessed this fight? How did you hear what was said?"

"It was at the Project Review Committee Meeting in City Hall. The Bay Area couple was against the project. And so was I. Afterward, when the City Council voted for the project, the Bay Area couple argued with Arthur outside in the parking lot. The husband must have pushed Arthur or tripped him because he was on the floor."

"Did anyone else witness this?"

"Everyone saw it. And the husband even said he would see Arthur dead first before letting mall goers traipse through his property. It was ugly." Peaches's face darkened. "Things will become ugly around here soon. So who stole my pie recipes?"

"Your sister, Michelle LaForge. How come her last name is slightly different than yours?"

Peaches closed her eyes, trying to hide her disappointment. "I knew it. Michelle is the youngest in our family. As a child, she was always pushing boundaries. She even changed her last name to LaForge when she got the job in Las Vegas. Some kind of headline dancer. I can't believe she would do this to me."

"I'm sorry. Sometimes family doesn't behave like we want them to."

The cry of a young child split the air. Raina spun and glanced in the direction of the barn. Was that Lila? Her heart rate sped up.

"New Rain! New Rain!"

By her niece's tone, Raina could tell Lila wasn't seriously hurt. Nevertheless, she sprinted for the barn with Peaches trailing her. When she rounded the corner of the house, she stopped in her tracks, and her jaw dropped open.

Lila toddled out of the barn, covered from head to toe in muck. Globs of brownish lumps with hay and other unmentionables trickled down her cherubic face. Her eyes were squeezed shut, and her mouth screamed her aunt's name. And standing next to her was an equally filthy Po Po with a sheepish expression on her face.

Raina blinked, but the image didn't go away. What the heck? Did the two of them wrestle with a pig?

"Oh, my..." The pie lady's laughter choked off the rest of her words.

Her husband grabbed a nearby hose and turned it on Raina's grandma and niece. The child's shrieks grew louder. She spotted Raina and ran full speed for her aunt.

Half a second after Lila buried her grimy face on Raina's legs, the scent of horse dung hit her sinuses. She opened her mouth to tell her niece it was okay, but a blast of water hit her in the face.

With her teeth chattering, Raina opened her trunk to pull out a microfleece blanket. She got Lila strapped into the car seat and wrapped the blanket around the child while breathing through her mouth.

Po Po sheepishly pulled a bath towel from her beach bag and laid it on the passenger seat before buckling herself in. She brushed a wet lock from her forehead and tossed a strand of hay out the window. She looked straight ahead, with all the dignity of the family matriarch.

Raina turned on the engine and cranked up the heat. The smell intensified, but there was nothing else she could do. "I want a full car detail."

"Done," Po Po said, still staring straight ahead.

"If this doesn't get rid of the smell, I want new upholstery."

"Done."

Raina pulled out of the driveway and onto the main road. She filled her grandma in on the conversation with the pie lady.

"If you're coming in from town, it's less driving to use the secondary access through the Rankins' property. You'd have to drive an extra half-mile to use the main entrance," Raina said.

"So the private road will become the de facto main entrance," Po Po said. "The Rankins wouldn't want the extra traffic. You can't live off the grid when you have all these cars going through your front yard."

"And don't forget the wear and tear on their half-million-dollar road. Even if Westchester Development helps pay for the repair, the Rankins wouldn't want construction in front of their house every few years."

Po Po shook her head. "Aledo and Sandra Rankin don't seem like the type of people to kill someone over an easement dispute though."

"It's not just an easement. It's the death of their dream retirement," Raina said grimly.

SOMEHOW RAINA MANAGED to get the three of them back to her grandma's condo complex. They left a trail of puddles and hay on the lobby floor on their way to the second floor. After dunking her niece in the tub and putting her in clean clothes, Raina made grilled cheese sandwiches for lunch.

She left her grandma and Lila during nap time for one of those car washes with a coin operated vacuum station. Even purchasing a pine tree freshener to hang on her rearview mirror didn't get rid of the smell. She drove to her apartment with the windows wide open, wishing she could have a do over to her morning. She showered and headed toward the offices of Westchester Development.

The building was a concrete tilt-up in an office complex, indistinguishable from its neighbors. The glass windows were darkly tinted so that she couldn't see anything inside, but she was sure occupants could see her clearly in the pale afternoon sunlight. Raina trotted up the brick steps, double-checked the address number—lucky eighty-eight—and entered the foyer. More than a few Chinese merchants had gone out of their way to ensure the numeral eight, which was a homonym for wealth, showed up in their businesses.

A receptionist manned the single curved desk in the waiting area. A set of mahogany double doors closed the rest of the office from prying eyes.

The perky blonde in the chic one-piece black dress looked familiar, but Raina couldn't recall her name. The blonde whispered into her cell phone and disconnected. She gave Raina a bright smile. "Hey, I know you. Raina Sun. My nephew is doing great, thanks to your grandma's help."

Raina blinked. Cora Campos? It had been two years since she last laid eyes on the student assistant for the history department. Where were the thick glasses and the baggy T-shirt? The Cora she knew looked more like a boney baby stork hiding among the furniture, not this self-assured cutie. Maybe she should ask for the number to Cora's fairy godmother because Raina needed a transformation before her wedding.

"Cora? When did you quit your job at the history department?" Raina asked.

"After the business over Holden's death. My boyfriend got me this job. The pay is much better, and I don't have to deal with Olivia anymore," Cora said.

Raina would jump over fiery coals herself to escape from Olivia, the monster boss. "How do you like working here? Is Arthur Westchester a good boss?"

The smile slipped from Cora's face. "I don't know if you heard. He died yesterday at one of his properties."

"Yes, I know." Raina pulled the invoice from her purse. "It's why I'm here. To collect on an outstanding bill that he still owed us."

Cora glanced at the paper. "Moody Investigation? Are you a private investigator now?"

"No, I'm not a private investigator. I do office work for Toni." All of which was technically true. "Do you know who I can talk to about collecting on this invoice? I want to make sure we're in line before the other creditors show up."

"I don't think you have to worry about other creditors. I don't know who to refer you to. Our office manager quit two weeks ago, and we haven't gotten a replacement yet. I guess you can talk to Arthur's partner, Robert Spillman. Let me go ask someone."

Cora locked her computer station and went through the double doors to the inner office. As soon as the receptionist was out of sight, Raina stepped around the desk and rifled through the drawer. Pens, sticky notes, and paper clips. Nothing of interest. As she shut the drawer, her hand bumped the tray underneath the desk, sending the wireless keyboard onto the floor. Smooth. Real smooth.

Raina dropped to her hands and knees to gather up the battery that fell out and the keyboard. She assembled it and slid it back on the tray. The glass front doors slid open, and voices tumbled in. She crawled under the desk, hoping the people would get inside before Cora came out.

"Where did Arthur get the idea?" a familiar voice asked. "Do you think he suspected anything?"

"If it makes you feel any better, he hired a private investigator on all his ex-wives, Mia," said a deep baritone voice.

"But he didn't die while he was married to them. The police are poking around my business, thinking I killed my husband," Mia said. "You've got to help me, Robert." Her voice wobbled at the end. "I had nothing to do with his death."

Raina didn't know if Mia was putting on an act, but her feminine appeal to Robert apparently worked.

"You have nothing to worry about. The prenup gives you nothing since your marriage didn't last the stipulated five years," he said.

"But what about Mateo's stupid stunt the other day—"

"Stop panicking. We have nothing to gain from Arthur's death. All you have is the house and the jewelry he bought you. I'll probably never see any return on my investment on the mall project. Without Arthur's influence and money, those stupid neighbors and the environmental group will stop the mall from going any further."

"Oh, honey, why couldn't we have met each other earlier?" Mia said, her voice full of regret.

"Stop it!" Robert hissed. "If you keep this up, the police will definitely have a reason to get into our business."

Raina's eyes widened. What the heck? Were the two of them having an affair? Talk about motive. A chirping sound filled the air, followed by a vibration from inside Raina's purse. Incoming text message.

8

A TANGLED WEB

Sweat broke out in the small of Raina's back, and her heart raced. Seriously? The one and only time she had a working cell phone in a murder investigation, and it gave her away. She resisted the urge to slam her purse on the tile floor.

Silence.

Raina's legs quivered with tension. She should get up and announce her presence. What could they do to her in broad daylight? Or maybe she should spray them with pepper spray and run out before they recognize her? But Cora would be able to identify Raina after she left the building. Raina took deep breaths to slow her racing heart. It didn't work.

"What was that?" Robert finally asked. He sounded nervous.

"Probably the receptionist's cell phone. Let's go into your office," Mia said.

"Let's not, Mia. We can't be seen together for a while. You're a grieving widow now."

"You're right as usual. I'll go home and wait until things die down. Do you think it'll be over in a couple of weeks?" Mia asked.

"We'll be lucky if everything gets settled by the end of the year," Robert said. "With no apparent heirs, everyone would be coming out of the woodwork with their hands out."

Mia gasped. "You're kidding."

"I'm afraid not, my dear. We'll have to be strangers for the next year." The front glass doors swooshed open. Footsteps approached. "Dad, I need to talk to you," a voice said. "Oh, hi, Mia..."

"Bobby," Robert said. There was a hint of a smile in his voice that wasn't there when he spoke to his lover.

"Robert Junior," Mia said. "I'll let the two of you have your manly chat."

"I heard about your husband. I'm sorry," Bobby blurted out. "If you need anything...you can always call me. I mean...you can call me even if you don't need anything."

"Uh, thanks," Mia said. Heels clicked on the tile floor, and glass doors swooshed open again.

Silence. Seconds ticked by.

"Son, she's not interested," Robert said. His baritone sounded troubled.

As he should be, Raina thought.

"If I need dating advice, I'll ask for it," Bobby said.

"Son, she's—"

"She's too good for a felon? Is that what you want to say?"

"She's married."

"Not anymore. And Mia was mine first before you sent me to prison."

Raina's eyes widened. *Prison*, she mouthed.

"Bobby, I didn't send you to jail. Your actions sent you there."

"Yeah, and you just let it happen. You know what? Nevermind. I don't even know why I'm here," Bobby said. Footsteps headed toward the glass doors. "You're always too busy—"

Footsteps followed Bobby. "Wait!"

"Keep your hands off me!" Bobby said.

Raina's cell phone rang again. Her fingers fumbled with the zipper of her purse.

"Who's here?" Bobby called out. Footsteps approached the desk.

"It's only the two of us. That's Cora's cell phone," Robert said.

"That's not Cora's ring tone," Bobby said.

A hot flash shot through Raina's body. Sweat poured out, and her hands shook. Her gaze drifted from her purse to a scowling pair of brown eyes. The jig was up.

"Who the hel—"

"Raina, what are you doing down there?" Cora strolled up next to Bobby.

"Good question," Robert said, joining the other two to stare underneath the desk. Raina identified him by the baritone in his voice.

"You know this woman?" Bobby asked Cora.

"Yes, she works for Moody Investigation. She's here to collect on Arthur's outstanding invoice," Cora said.

"A private investigator?" Robert asked.

"No, she works in the office," Cora said.

Raina closed her eyes, hoping this was a bad dream. *One Mississippi. Two Mississippi.*

Her cell phone pinged to let her know the caller left a voicemail. Nope. She was caught red-handed. She couldn't even say she was looking for an earring because she didn't wear any jewelry. She took her time crawling out from underneath the desk.

Maybe she should go on the offensive by asking questions and ignoring the uncomfortable dilemma of why she was under Cora's desk. Or maybe she should act loony, so they would think she was an eccentric like her grandma. She ran her hand through her curly black hair, hoping to fluff it up, so she looked half crazed. Most people ignored crazies because it made them uncomfortable.

"Sorry, I was snooping in Cora's desk," Raina said, averting her gaze. "I was looking for information on other creditors who might have first dibs." The excuse sounded lame even to her ears, but she didn't dare to tell the truth with potential murder suspects in the room.

Cora gasped. "Raina!"

"Sorry, we're a mom-and-pop shop. We can't afford to work for free," Raina said.

The two men didn't share Cora's shock. They studied Raina with suspicion. Robert took a step back, crossing his arms over his paunch and avoiding eye contact. He probably figured Raina heard his entire conversation with Mia. Bobby, on the other hand, had the squinty-eye mean look of an animal waiting to pounce. The man had a chip the size of Mount Everest on his shoulder, and Raina wanted nothing to do with it.

Both men were tall and well-muscled, but Robert was forty pounds too heavy. They both shared brown eyes and sandy brown hair, although Robert had more silver in his.

"Cora, take the invoice. We'll issue a check within thirty days," Robert said.

Raina handed over the invoice. She shifted from foot to foot. With the three of them staring at her, she felt like a roach under a microscope.

"Anything else?" Robert asked, raising an eyebrow. His tone was caustic.

"Thank you for your time," Raina said and slunk toward the glass doors. She took her time leaving, hoping Robert and his son would resume their conversation. When it was clear no one was talking with her in the building, Raina hightailed it to the parking lot.

Once in her car, Raina leaned her forehead on the steering wheel. She took a few deep breaths. The faint muck smell was still in the air but there wasn't much she could do about it.

What happened inside Westchester Development

was too close for comfort. It was one thing to investigate a murder in the peripheral, but her link to Moody Investigation would naturally make people assume she was involved. Being a PI might become a liability, especially if she wanted to continue to help Matthew in the future.

Granted, it would be a couple more years before she would have enough field hours to qualify for the exam. But she was afraid if she committed to go down this path it wouldn't end up where she wanted to go. Being a grown-up was complicated.

She pulled out her cell phone and checked her text message. It was from Po Po.

Got an idea on how to ID the kidnapper. Practicing dance for Trunk-or-Treat. Come to SC to discuss.

Raina checked the voicemail. Her grandma had left a similar message. Great. She almost peed her pants because Po Po got a brain burp.

Knock! Knock!

Raina gasped and dropped her phone. It slid in the gap between the seat and the center console. She glanced at the driver side window. Bobby stood on the outside, giving her a wide car salesman smile. She turned the key in the ignition and rolled down the window a few inches. No way was she opening it wide enough for him to reach inside.

"Sorry I startled you," Bobby said. He slid a business card through the window. "Bobby Spillman of Spillman Insurance. I want to give you my card. Do you need rental insurance? I give a good discount for college students."

Raina blinked at him. Spillman Insurance? Could this be her grandma's insurance agent? "Do you sell burial insurance too?"

Bobby's smile didn't change, but he leaned back from the window. "Yes, I do, but only to senior citizens. I take care of special requests like scattering the ashes into the ocean or on a mountaintop. I take care of final arrangements so the surviving families can get on with their lives." He squinted at her. "You're too young to be thinking about burial insurance."

"I'm thinking of my grandma," she said, which was technically true. She leaned closer to the window. "Is your father also a partner at Spillman Insurance? Wow, he must be a busy guy."

Bobby shook his head. "I started the business a few years ago, but it has nothing to do with my father." His smile wavered. "He is always too busy, but we're not here to discuss my family."

Raina hoped she gave him an encouraging look. Oh, she so wanted to talk about his family. "At least he's still around. My dad has been gone for over a decade, and I still miss him."

"Family, they sure have a way of messing us up," Bobby said. "So about insurance...homeowner insurance on a rental property doesn't cover a tenant's personal items. If your unit catches on fire, you'll lose everything in your home. You can't afford to not have rental insurance."

Raina thought about Bobby's statement. Most of her furniture was hand-me-downs and could be replaced by asking around in her family again. And her laptop was backed up to the cloud. So in reality, she would only need to buy new clothes and toiletries. The only irreplaceable thing in her apartment was the gold gilded koi clock from Matthew, and insurance would be no help there.

"How come your father isn't a partner in your business but has a partnership with Arthur Westchester?"

Bobby shrugged and backed away from her car. "I have to meet a client. Give me a call the next time you're shopping for insurance."

Raina watched him get into his white BMW SUV. It looked identical to Mia's.

Raina gave him a wave when he drove by her car on the way out of the parking lot. She opened her car door and dug under the car seat for her cell phone. She replied to her grandma's text message.

I'LL BE THERE LATER. I HAVE A MEETING WITH DS.

Her grandma replied immediately.

DON'T MAKE IT EASY ON HIM.

Raina snorted at the message. She should wait until she had her grandma for backup, but someone had to keep an eye on her niece. She looked up the address on her phone. It was for a diner by the railroad tracks. She hoped they had pumpkin spice muffins. As she pulled out onto the street, she thought about what she heard at Westchester Development.

What a strange love triangle. Or would it be quadrangle in this case?

First, there was the December-May marriage between Arthur and Mia Westchester. Then, there was the December-May love affair between Robert Spillman Senior and Mia Westchester. Did she have a thing for older men?

And finally, there was the one-sided crush between Robert Spillman Junior a.k.a. Bobby and Mia Westchester. Mia had to be aware Bobby was in love with her. A woman like her must feel a man's desire like a beacon.

Raina chewed her lower lip. She remembered something else. Bobby made a comment that sounded like he used to have a relationship with Mia before his incarceration. And he blamed his father for sending him to jail. What was that about? There might be court documents on his felony. She made a mental note to do a little research the next time she was at Moody Investigation.

9

A FAILED BLACKMAIL

As Raina watched Detective Sokol slurp his chocolate milkshake, she tried not to cringe at their surroundings. They were seated in a duct-taped booth at Lousy Larry's Burgers. The grime on the table was worse than any hole-in-the-wall restaurant in Chinatown. If she caught a disease from this place, could she send the medical bill to the police department?

"As I was saying, I am glad you're on the case, Ms. Sun," Detective Sokol said.

"Thank you?" Raina wasn't sure if he was being facetious. She kept her elbows close to her body. She wasn't touching anything unless necessary. "The Venus Café is only a few blocks from the police station. It's a drive to get here."

"That place is too rich for my blood. Don't you remember I have new twin boys?" He reached for his wallet.

"I've seen their photos. You keep flashing them every time you want something from me. What do you want this time?"

Detective Sokol chuckled like they were old friends sharing an inside joke. "Ms. Sun, you're hilarious. We should have more Good Samaritans like you in this town, who are willing to help the police. You should think about applying to be a volunteer deputy."

"Sorry, I don't have time. I need to work for a living."

Detective Sokol shrugged. "Maybe after you marry Matthew Louie, you'll have more time."

Raina glared at him. Whenever he mentioned Matthew, she couldn't help but feel like there was a knife behind her back. She ignored his comment. "Did the autopsy report for Arthur Winchester come in yet?"

"Yeah, murder, as I suspected. A blow to the back of the head, which probably knocked him onto the rake."

Raina sat back in the booth. Just as he suspected, huh? At least there was official confirmation there was foul play. "Where did the rake come from? He didn't seem like the type to do yard work."

"No idea. The wife never saw it before either. It could have come from the local hardware store or one of the big box stores. We don't have the resources to follow up on this."

"So you're not doing anything?"

"The rake is not an easily identifiable antique. What do you expect me to do? Go door-to-door from here to Sacramento and ask if they sold a rake to a mustache-twirling bad guy?"

Raina glared at him. He had a point. "Any prints on the rake? Any nicks?"

"Just Arthur's prints. It's brand new. Not even a scratch on it."

Either the killer brought a brand new rake to the old pumpkin patch to kill Arthur with it, or Arthur brought the rake to the site himself. It doesn't make sense for the rake to be a weapon of choice when a gun or knife could be easily concealed until the fatal moment. So Arthur must have brought the rake to the site. Was he trying to dig up something?

"I can hear the gears churning in that pretty head of yours," Detective Sokol said. "Do you mind sharing what you're thinking?"

Her grandma's words came back to her. She shouldn't make it easy for him. Looking out for the police department didn't mean handing Detective Sokol the case in a bow. And she didn't like his tone. "Why should I help you? I'm not even a professional."

"Look, the chief is retiring at the end of the year. Matthew and I are the only two candidates for the promotion. And we both know Matthew doesn't want it, so this leaves me." His chest puffed up like a rooster. "I could be your beloved's new boss in a few months. Either you help me to serve justice, or I can make someone's life a living hell when I'm in charge. Do you understand what I'm saying?"

Raina wanted to slap the smirk off his face. Talk

about counting chicks before the eggs hatched. No way was this jerk going to be her fiancé's boss. Whether Matthew wanted it or not, he would be the next police chief if she had her way. And this jerk in front of her would be collateral damage after her grandma was done with him. "Crystal clear."

Detective Sokol's smile widened, and he rubbed his hands together. "Now what do you have for me? I know you've been a busy bee because you are annoying Joanna Hopper."

Raina opened her mouth to protest but closed it when the server slid a platter of bacon cheeseburger and fries in front of the detective. She leaned away from the rancid grease, hoping she wouldn't throw up.

Detective Sokol happily drowned his fries in ketchup. Her grandma was much the same with food, but she was in her seventies and exercised every day. This Danny DeVito doppelgänger didn't have a fighting chance against the salt and fat.

"Let me guess. You're not a donut guy," Raina said.

"I prefer salt. Larry makes the best burgers. The name was supposed to be a joke, but horrible for business. He's my brother-in-law," the detective said.

Raina nodded to acknowledge his words, but she wasn't trying Larry's food without more incentive. "Did you find anything else about the case? What did you learn from the Rankins?"

"Lovely couple, but a few loose screws, if you know what I mean."

"I don't know," Raina said. City people pretending to be farmers weren't unusual.

"Who would sink half a million into the farm they bought? There's a reason the fields have been fallow for years." He whirled a finger around the side of his head. "Crazy rich people, that's who."

"I don't think they're rich. It's their entire life's savings."

"Even worse then. They should have bought a nice condo in a retirement community. They don't need to take on this kind of risk at their age."

For once she agreed with him. "At least they're chasing a dream. Not too many people get that opportunity these days."

"Why the interest in them? The Rankins can't be the murderers. They might be crazy dreamers, but I don't think they are stupid. They wouldn't dispose of the body so close to their home, especially after a public argument with the victim over an access easement."

Raina blinked. She hadn't expected the detective to put this much thought into the case already. His appearance and personality might hide a sharp mind. She should be more careful around him. After all, there was still a chance he could be Matthew's future boss. "Did they talk about anything else besides the body discovery?"

"Like what?"

"Gossip?"

He gave her a disgusted look. "I don't have time to be a therapist."

So he didn't bother asking if they'd heard or seen anything unusual leading up to the body discovery. Raina would need to get out to the Rankins' farm and have a conversation with them. If nothing else, she could try to recruit Aledo Rankin to be a volunteer deputy for the police department. This ought to make Matthew's current boss happy, thereby increasing his chances of getting the promotion for chief.

"Why do you have that cheesy grin on your face?" the detective asked.

"Sorry. I was just thinking about Matthew. Is there anything else we need to discuss here? I'm in a hurry to pick up my niece."

Detective Sokol waved dismissively. "Just keep me in the loop if you discover anything. Don't try to take down the murderer on your own. You'll need a trained professional for this."

Raina slid out of the booth. A monkey could be a trained professional. But Officer Joanna Hopper had more sense than the jerk in front of her. She couldn't believe he tried to blackmail her into helping him.

RAINA LEFT Detective Sokol to finish his food and headed toward the senior center. She would have to wait until Monday to use the Moody Investigation computer to run Bobby Spillman's name through the various databases unavailable to her at home.

Unlike her other cases, the suspects on this one were starting to pile up. First, there were Aledo and Sandra Rankin. They had sunk their entire savings into creating a farming co-op, never realizing the adjacent pumpkin field would develop into a shopping mall. They had a public argument with Arthur Westchester over using their private road as a secondary access road to a new mall in their backyard. They certainly had a motive and access to the victim.

Then, there was Mia Westchester who—

Raina paused. Maybe Mia Westchester shouldn't be on the suspect list. With a prenuptial agreement, she would be better off financially with her husband alive. Granted, there was the affair with Robert Spillman, but she could divorce her husband at any time and be no worse off than now. The kidnapping was another puzzle, but it might have nothing to do with Arthur's death.

But what about Robert Spillman? Maybe he didn't like his lady love to go home to somebody else? A crime of passion? This was a plausible motive and one that satisfied her grandma's love for drama.

Finally, there was Bobby. At the moment he seemed to have daddy issues more than anything else. While he may carry a torch for Mia, killing her husband wouldn't gain him anything because she wasn't interested in the first place. His motive was murky at best unless he killed Arthur for "stealing"

Mia while he was in prison. This was a stretch. But he stayed on the suspect list until she could eliminate him from it.

Raina felt sorry for the guy. Bobby didn't even know he never had a chance with Mia. How would he react when he found out his father and Mia were having an affair?

Unfortunately, most of the suspects knew Raina worked for Moody Investigations. And if the Rankins spoke to their neighbor, they would eventually find out about her link to the only private investigator in town.

Even more troubling, Raina wasn't sure how Toni would react once she found out Raina had been investigating the case and using the invoice collection as an excuse to check out the suspects.

10

HEY, SEXY LADY

Raina blinked at the flyer posted on the community bulletin board next to the entrance of the senior center recreation room. "Have you seen me?" graced the top of the flyer. Underneath the heading was a sketch of the kidnapper. It further explained the man was on medication and his aunt was looking for him. There was the contact info for a five-hundred-dollar reward.

Was this her grandma's brilliant idea? She double-checked the contact number, but it wasn't one of her grandma's phone numbers. What the heck? Was somebody else also looking for the kidnapper? Maybe this was Mia Westchester's doing.

Raina glanced behind her. There wasn't anyone around. She grabbed the flyer and stuffed it into her purse. The case kept getting stranger by the minute.

Music thumped from behind the closed doors. Raina couldn't make out the song, but it was more hippie hoppy than jazzy. She couldn't believe her grandma and her friends—aka The Posse Club—would dance in the talent show during the Trunk-or-Treat event next week. They were all over sixty, and people their age usually didn't groove like they used to. With her grandma, Raina wasn't sure what to expect. She cracked open the door, and her jaw dropped.

"Hey, sexy lady!" the speakers blared.

Six senior women and two senior men lip-synced and gyrated to *Gangnam Style*. Po Po had on a teal-colored tuxedo jacket with black slacks and a black bow tie. Why was Raina not surprised her grandma was the lead dancer? Frank Small, her grandma's wingman, had on a skinny yellow tuxedo, a toupee, and yellow sneakers. The rest of the ladies were in seventies geometric disco dresses with knee-high go-go boots. The other man in the group had on a tank top, Bermuda shorts, and a life vest. Even her little niece had on several pieces of bling and dark sunglasses. It was obvious the child couldn't see because she kept bumping into the adults while she pranced around like a horse. They were the oddest dance group Raina had ever seen, and yet it worked.

There were two other senior citizens in the audience. One of them was Janice Tally, her grandma's arch nemesis. Her fingers gripped the walker in front of her, and her lips disappeared into her frown. She would probably petition the social committee to ban her grandma and her friends from the talent show once she left the room.

Raina joined the small audience. She was close enough to hear somebody's hip pop, but the dancer just winced and continued to shuffle with the beat. Geez, these ladies wanted to win the talent show pretty badly.

At the end of the song, instead of pointing at the sky like in the music video, The Posse Club pointed at the audience and pulled the trigger on party poppers. Streamers shot out at the audience, covering their heads and shoulders.

Raina put her fingers in her mouth and whistled. "Woohoo! Go, ladies!"

Po Po blushed until her cheeks matched the pink streaks in her hair. Lila bounced up and down, clapping her hands. The folks in this town were in for a surprise. Raina didn't think Halloween would be the same after this performance.

An hour later, Raina brought out plates of chicken breasts and roasted potatoes to the dining room table in her grandma's condo. Po Po and Lila tucked into their food as if they'd done manual labor all day. Raina filled her grandma in on everything that happened since she dropped them off for nap time.

"A love triangle! This is even better than a cabana boy. Somebody must have gotten jealous. A crime of passion," Po Po said.

"I don't think so," Raina said. "Mia could divorce Arthur any time, and she doesn't appear to care about Bobby anymore. She's with Robert now."

"Lila done. TV time?" her niece asked.

Po Po got the child settled in the living room while Raina cleaned up the dining room table. They reconvened fifteen minutes later over cups of green tea at the table. Raina pulled out her notebook to finish her notes for the case.

"Did you see my handiwork at the senior center?" Po Po asked.

"The performance was great," Raina said, pulling out the Wanted flyer with the sketch of the kidnapper on it. "Did you see this?"

"Yeah! That's my handiwork," Po Po said, beaming.

"Where did you get this? The sketch looks like it came from a police sketch artist."

"One of my high school kids. I paid her another hundred dollars to make copies and to post the flyer around town." Po Po sat back and rested her hands behind her head. "Am I smart or what?"

"This is genius! I can't believe I didn't even think of it."

"Well, you know what they say about the apple on the tree, but you're not so bad yourself, Rainy."

Raina blinked. Was this a compliment or a compliment to her grandma? She shook her head. Never mind. It wasn't worth the mental effort. "Do you think anyone would believe you're looking for your nephew? The kidnapper didn't seem like he was on medication."

"It doesn't matter. Someone will still want the reward. A call will come in sooner or later with all the starving students in this town." Po Po slid a prepaid cell phone to Raina. "Keep this close. The call will come in on it."

Raina stared at the phone. What were the odds? Not only would she have a cell phone for this case, now she would have two. Her ancestors must enjoy this joke.

"I'm going to the Rankins' farm tomorrow to have a chat with them." She hesitated. After what happened at the pie lady's farm, she wasn't sure if her grandma should be allowed in someone's home. "Do you want to come along?"

Po Po shook her head. "Rainy, we should just ask Arthur who killed him. What we need is a Chinese séance at the old pumpkin patch."

"We can't have a séance. We don't have a blind Chinese woman."

"Oh, yes we do, my dear girl. We have Maggie Louie," Po Po said, her voice brimming with triumph.

"She's not blind."

"She's getting there. That's good enough."

Raina smacked her palm on her forehead. "We're not dragging Matthew's half-blind grandma to the pumpkin patch and asking her to read the markings on ancient coins. We don't even have the right paraphernalia for this." She couldn't imagine what she'd say to her fiancé if his grandma stumbled and fell.

"Actually, I have a tortoise shell and the ancient coins. They belonged to my mother. It'll be okay. We'll hold onto Maggie and make sure she doesn't fall."

"She's not trained to interpret the omens."

Po Po shrugged. "It comes from the divine. I'm sure she'll manage to read it or make something up."

"And how will making something up help us with this case?"

"The cosmos will align to help us. You'll see."

Raina rubbed her temples. Her grandma was being obtuse on purpose. Did she need an assignment for her cronies at the senior center? "Absolutely not."

Po Po jutted out her lower lip. "Then what brilliant idea do you have?"

Raina raised an eyebrow at the challenge in her grandma's voice. "I'll recruit Aledo for the volunteer deputy position."

"You can't do that. You're not authorized to represent the police."

"I'm a concerned citizen. With the murder rate in this town, I'm doing my civic duty by recruiting volunteers."

Po Po snorted. "You're just trying to win kudos for Matthew."

Raina ignored her grandma's comment. "You don't even believe in séances."

"How do you know I don't? I was born and raised in China, the land of dragons and ancestral ghosts. My culture is an integral part of me. You're too Americanized to understand this."

Raina paused, considering her grandma's words. She'd never thought much about her grandma's youth beyond the few tidbits that made her legendary in their family.

She knew her grandmother was the only child of a third wife, who was a Chinese opera singer. She was abandoned by her mother as a young child and was kicked out of the family when her father died in her late teens. And somehow she ended up in Hong Kong and met Raina's grandfather. After their marriage, they immigrated to San Francisco and built their family business.

It was a life so removed from her own that she'd never given it much thought. Maybe she should encourage her grandma to talk about it.

"Do you resent your mother? For abandoning you?" Raina whispered.

Po Po sipped her tea, taking so long Raina thought her grandma didn't hear her. "Do you resent your mom for abandoning you after your dad died?"

Raina blinked. Her mom didn't abandon her. She retreated...she abdicated her role as a parent... No, there was no abandonment.

"It's the same," Po Po said, almost as if reading Raina's thoughts. "Melody moved back into my home and spent years in bed while you and your siblings grew up."

"But she was still there, and she had to get over her broken heart. She didn't have a choice."

"Even at six, I knew my mother would have to leave, or the other wives would kill her eventually after she fell out of favor because she had me."

Raina's eyes widened. "What?"

"Metaphorically speaking. My mother was too

modern for the time. They would have locked her away in a room, forgotten and ignored except for cere-monial events. Eventually, the opium would have gotten her," Po Po said flatly.

Raina glanced down at her teacup, blinking back tears. After her childhood, the rest of her grandma's life must be a living rainbow in comparison. "Mom had to do what she did to survive my dad's death. I was an adult then, so I didn't need her."

Po Po patted Raina's hand. "You were seventeen. Your brother was still in elementary school. And we don't even want to start on Cassie's Barbie doll world. Of course the three of you needed your mother. I tried to do the best I could..." Her voice cracked. "But I'm an old woman..."

Raina threw her arms around her grandma, pulling the tiny woman into a tight hug. Tears ran down her face, wetting her grandma's shoulders. They held each other this way for a long moment, sobbing and lost in their thoughts.

"New Rain, hungry," Lila's childish voice said. The patter of tiny feet crossed the wood floors, and a hand tugged on Raina's shirt. "Hungry."

Raina pulled away from her grandma, wiping at her face.

"Owie, New Rain?" Lila said, lower lip jutting out. "Tai Po owie?"

Raina gave the child a wobbly smile. "You mean my Po Po."

"No, my Tai Po," Lila said, raising her voice.

"No, she's mine. So she's my Po Po."

Lila giggled at the game. Po Po was the formal title for a maternal grandma, and Tai Po was the formal title for maternal great-grandma. If Raina let her, Lila would play this game for the next few minutes.

Po Po stood, a hand on her hip. "I don't know who the two of you are calling grandma. I'm young and hip." She tossed her head. "I even have pink hair. I'm more like your mommy."

Lila scrunched up her face with her hands until wrinkles appeared. "No, Tai Po. You're too old to be Mommy."

Raina burst out laughing, and she clasped her hands over her mouth. She couldn't contain her mirth, and her breaths came out in snorts.

Po Po gave her a dirty look. "Someday, this will be you."

Raina got up and went to the kitchen, her shoulders still shaking with laughter. The brutal honesty of children knew no bounds.

As she cut an apple for Lila, Raina sighed. She was glad they stopped talking about her mother. She didn't have mommy issues, and done was done. There wasn't a thing she could do to make Mom pay attention to her.

Raina jerked. A drop of blood beaded on her finger. This was what happened when she didn't pay attention to the task at hand. She stuck the finger in her mouth and returned to the dining room. She slid the plate over to the child happily nestled on Po Po's lap.

"Why don't we try recruiting Aledo Rankin first?" Raina said, returning to their earlier conversation. "The séance can be the backup plan. Besides, you'll need time to assemble everything anyway."

Po Po pretended to think it over, tapping her chin with a finger.

"Then you're flying solo tomorrow morning, Rainy. I will have to prepare for Operation Ghostbuster."

Raina sagged with relief. *Hallelujah!* She better get the information she needed from the Rankins because there was no way she was resorting to Operation Ghostbuster to get her answers.

11

———

OPEN SEASON

fter tucking Lila in for the evening, Raina went back to her apartment to shower and call Matthew. She stared at the ceiling fan above her bed while she filled him in, leaving out the part where Detective Sokol threatened to make Matthew's life miserable if he got the promotion. Her fiancé would only laugh and dismiss the entire thing as a joke.

"I'm worried Toni will end the internship. Is this a sign?" Raina asked.

"A sign of what?" Matthew asked over the phone.

She pressed her forearm on her forehead, blocking out the ceiling light. "I don't know. Maybe I'm not meant to be a private investigator."

He was silent for several moments. The whir of the ceiling fan lulled her senses until her eyes grew heavy. It had been a long day.

"It can be a dangerous profession," he finally said.

"We can't have both parents in this family facing down criminals every day."

She sat up, trying to digest what he said. They hadn't set a wedding date, but he was already talking about starting a family. Cart before the horse much? "What happened to you opening a private investigation company?"

While she had initially rejected working for him, she might not have another option if Toni no longer wanted an apprentice. Besides, how bad could it be to work with her husband? They could spend twenty-four hours together.

"No, you were right. It's not feasible. I need the benefits and a steady paycheck."

"If you're thinking about me, I can earn my keep. There's no need for you to give up on a dream on my account."

"I know you can. But I like being able to provide for my family. It might not be the two of us forever. And I also have to think about my grandma."

"Okay, what the heck happened in San Francisco? Where is my fiancé? Because you're not him. He wouldn't even commit to a wedding date a few days ago," Raina said. Her tone was light and teasing, but she was serious. Where did all of this come from?

"One of your cousins announced her engagement a few days ago. All the aunts and female cousins are flitting around her and making a big fuss about it. It just made me realize my Rainy deserves just as much attention."

Raina blinked rapidly at the tears in her eyes. He did change. She swallowed, not trusting her voice. She had been waiting for the other shoe to drop for months. While she never voiced it, she had been expecting him to break off their engagement all this time.

Her chest swelled with joy, and a wide smile broke out on her face. He meant it. They were getting married! When she replied, her voice was thick with emotion. "Are we setting a date?"

"How's next September? This will be a few months after your cousin's wedding, so we don't have to worry about stealing her thunder."

She closed her eyes, tears streaming down her face. "A…" She swallowed. "A Chinese wedding?" She suppressed the urge to kick up her legs and laugh.

"I don't think our grandmas would let us get away with anything less."

It wasn't until after they hung up that Raina realized she hadn't bothered to ask which one of her cousins got engaged.

She spent the night tossing and turning over their conversation. September was less than a year away, and a Chinese wedding needed a full year to plan. From her side of the family, there were probably three hundred guests already. What did she get herself into?

When Raina got up for her morning run, she decided her grandma could take the reins. The only decision she wanted to make was the dress and the venue. Po Po would have a ball. Besides, Raina didn't want to fight with her mother. Much easier to let Po Po pull rank to get her mother in line.

After she got back, and while she was showering, she remembered she needed to have a chat with Officer Hopper. Now that Detective Sokol laid his cards on the table, it was in everyone's best interests to keep him from becoming chief.

THE NEXT MORNING, armed with nothing more than Matthew's business card, Raina drove to the Rankins' farm. With the driver side window down and the scent of apples and smoke in the air, Raina found it difficult to reconcile the picturesque landscape with the heinous murder a few days ago.

Arthur Westchester was once a living, breathing man, but now he would never taste a crisp fall apple again. And even more shocking, no one seemed to care. Not his wife. Not his business partner. This was sad—to live a life with no one to grieve your death. She took a deep breath, hoping to dislodge her melancholy mood.

The Rankins owned over a hundred acres. Plenty of room for a farming co-op. At the intersection of the main road and private road to the Rankins' driveway, a red "For Sale" sign beckoned passing vehicles. When did their property come on the market?

Raina pulled over and got out of the car. She grabbed a flyer from the stack in the plastic case nailed to the signpost. There was nothing unusual in the listing, though there was no mention of the access easement. Who would buy the property with an ongoing murder investigation in the next field? Nobody local for sure.

She got back into the car and drove to the farmhouse. The porch area was swept, and potted flowers were placed strategically next to the swing. A bright "Welcome Home" garden sign greeted buyers next to the front door. She pressed the doorbell and strains of a lilting melody with a waterfall background filled the air. The Rankins couldn't have staged the home more perfectly.

The front door swung open, and Sandra Rankin beamed at Raina. She had sable brown hair and warm brown eyes with fair skin that wasn't made for a farming life. There wasn't a hint of gray in her mane, so she either had a good hairstylist or she plucked out the white hairs. Even though she was of average height, Raina still had to look up at her.

"Hi, the showing isn't for another hour. Our realtor isn't even here yet," Sandra said.

Raina returned the smile. "Hi, my name is Raina Sun, and I work for a private investigation office. Your neighbor Peaches La Fargo asked us to find the person who sold her secret pie recipe. Do you mind if I ask you a few questions?"

"I'm not sure how much I can tell you. And I don't have a lot of time. I need to finish prepping the house before the showing." Sandra held onto the doorknob to prevent Raina from peeking inside her house.

"It'll only take a few minutes. Have you noticed any new people in your neighborhood?"

"No."

"Have you noticed any kind of argument next door?"

"No."

Raina wanted to sigh in frustration. The person in front of her wasn't going to volunteer anything. Time to change tactics. She glanced down at her notebook, pretending to consult her notes. "When was the last time you saw Arthur Westchester?" She glanced up in time to see Sandra forcing her clenched jaw to relax. Oops, she must have hit a nerve.

"What does Arthur Westchester have to do with pies?"

"He's a neighbor, and when it comes to corporate espionage, I'm sure he has plenty of experience."

Sandra gaped at Raina. "I hope this is not your day job because you need to check your facts first, girl. Arthur Westchester died a few days ago."

Raina widened her eyes in pretend shock. "Oh, no. Did he have health issues? Was it an accident?" She hoped she played the young and dumb card right.

Sandra shrugged. "Who knows? The man was a jerk."

"So he was a cranky guy?"

"No, he was as nice as can be. Very charming with old school breeding and money."

Raina cocked her head. "I'm confused. How could he be both charming and a jerk?"

"He assumed he would get his way. I didn't like dealing with him."

"Are you talking about the access road issue on your property? Is this why you're selling your house?"

Sandra blinked as if regretting how much she said. "You're not here to listen to neighborhood gossip. I don't know who stole Peaches' recipes. She seemed like the kind of woman who might make this up for the attention."

Raina frowned, pretending to do some heavy mental gymnastics. "It must be mighty convenient that Arthur Westchester died," she continued, ignoring Sandra's comment. "You didn't have anything to do with his death, did you?"

Sandra's mouth opened and closed as she processed what Raina said. "I don't have to tell you anything."

"Sorry, sometimes I get a little nosy. It's a small town pastime. I hope the police didn't frighten you with their questioning. I'm from the Bay Area too, and I've seen how this police force does their job."

"I knew it! I told Aledo that Danny DeVito look-alike would try to frame us."

"I'm sure you have nothing to hide...but it looks bad because you're trying to get out of town."

A bead of sweat appeared on Sandra's temple. "We had already decided to put the property on the market before Arthur's death. Our realtor can verify this. I'm tired of the stupid punks and the stress from the mall. This isn't how I envisioned my retirement. We're moving to Texas where we can get more land for our money."

Raina studied Sandra. If the Rankins started the process to put their house on the market before Arthur Westchester's death, they would have no motive for killing him. Her gut believed Sandra, and a quick call to their realtor would verify their story.

"Before you move, does Aledo want to work as a volunteer deputy for the police force?" Raina asked.

Sandra stared at Raina as if her brain were leaking onto her shoulders. "Not a chance."

Raina sighed. At least she could cross the Rankins off the suspect list.

Sandra frowned and stiffened. She cupped a hand behind her right ear.

"Are you—"

"Shhh!"

Raina strained to hear what caught Sandra's attention. A chime rang out, crystal clear in the silence. Was that a bell and chanting?

"Do you hear that?" Sandra whispered.

Raina nodded, wondering why they were whispering.

Sandra reached inside the house and grabbed a jacket. She threw it on and trotted toward the pickup truck parked in the driveway. "I gotta go. The punks are back again, and this time I got my rifle ready."

An uneasy fluttering settled into Raina's stomach.

Who were the punks, and why would they ring a bell and chant like...a séance? She ran after Sandra, grabbing the handle of the passenger side door. "Can I come with you? This is the most excitement I've seen all month." She climbed in, reaching for the seat belt.

"Just stay out of my way. Aledo and I are sick and tired of picking up beer cans and trash on our property," Sandra said, backing out from the driveway. She threw the gear into drive, and it shot off down toward the private road that ran along the edge of the property.

Raina held onto the grab bars on the dash as the pickup took off. She glanced at the rifle in the console between the seats. "Just talk before you shoot. I have a feeling these punks might be my grandma and her friends."

12

MORE THAN BABY BACK...RIBS?

Even from several hundred feet away, Raina could make out three people with black silk Chinese pajamas standing around a TV dinner tray in the old pumpkin patch. Sandra parked behind Frank Small's gray Subaru on her private road.

"What is going on here?" Sandra asked, squinting over the dash of her truck. "You can't have a costume party at a crime scene."

Raina groaned inwardly. On the bright side, no one was reaching for a shotgun. "My grandma wanted to call up Arthur's ghost to find out who killed him. What you're seeing is a Chinese séance..." Raina paused, considering her words. "Actually, it's more like amateur hour. Think *Saturday Night Live*."

"Doesn't a séance need to happen at night in a dark room? And the man isn't even Chinese," Sandra said, pointing at Frank. His dark brown skin glistened in the pale afternoon sunlight.

"He's an honorary Chinese."

"Which one is your grandma?"

"The one with pink streaks in her white hair."

Sandra smirked at Raina. "Go figure. The apple didn't fall far from the family tree, huh?"

Raina ignored the comment and hopped out of the car. She wasn't sure if the comment was a compliment or an insult, and she didn't care enough to pursue it. "Let's see if they found anything."

"Probably more beer cans."

As the truck doors slammed shut, Frank glanced over and froze. His hand darted out and grabbed Po Po's sleeve. She brushed him off. He rested his large hands on her shoulders, turning her until she faced Raina and Sandra. A guilty expression crossed her grandma's face, and she gave them a small finger wave. Maggie Louie turned to face them, but Raina knew they appeared to be nothing more than blurred shapes to the visually impaired woman.

"Can we do the good cop-bad cop? I want to scare my grandma, so she doesn't pull another stunt like this again. I told her this would be a bad idea," Raina whispered.

"Okay, let me grab my rifle," Sandra said, reaching into the cab of the truck.

"No, no. We don't need an actual gun."

Sandra winked. "I think we should have a little fun with this." She slung the rifle over her shoulder and marched toward Po Po and her cronies.

Raina trotted to keep up with Sandra's longer legs.

When they got within hearing distance, Sandra yelled, "What the heck is going on here? You better not be having an orgy on my neighbor's property."

Frank glanced at the rifle, licking his lower lip. "No, ma'am. We're here to investigate the murder."

"Are you with the police?" Sandra asked.

"No, ma'am. We're Good Samaritans," Frank said.

Sandra jerked her thumb at Raina. "You mean a nosy Samaritan like this one."

Everyone turned to study Raina. "I thought you were supposed to be foaming at the mouth and scaring the pants off these Good Samaritans," Raina whispered.

"Why do I have to play the bad guy?" Sandra asked.

Raina glanced at the rifle and back at Sandra. She should have known better than to count on a D-rated actress. "What's on the tray?"

Someone had laid a gold brocade cloth on top of the TV dinner tray. Po Po and her cronies didn't even look up from their intent study of the items on top of the tray. It held a tortoise shell, a few ancient coins, and a bone fragment.

"We found a bone when we were pacing out ley lines for the séance," Po Po said.

Raina raised an eyebrow. Ley lines? What did her grandma know about the supernatural and the mystic?

As if sensing Raina's doubt, Po Po tipped up her chin. "I have friends in high places."

Raina had the same friends. They shared the same ancestors after all, but she didn't go around pretending to be a mystic. Did her grandma believe in this or did she believe in it when it was convenient?

"We're trying to figure out which animal the bone came from," Frank cut in.

"Let me see," Sandra said, extending her hand.

Frank handed her the bone.

Sandra sucked in a breath, and her hand shook. "This didn't come from an animal. It's a human rib bone."

Po Po frowned. "Are you sure?"

"I used to be a registered nurse. Yes, I'm sure," Sandra said.

"Are there more?" Raina asked, wincing at the squeak in her voice.

Frank and Po Po shared a look. "We should call the police."

After making the call, Sandra drove back to her house to wait for the realtor. She didn't want to go, but an Open House wasn't something she could ignore. She promised to come back as soon as she could.

Raina suspected Sandra wanted firsthand knowledge so she could tell her friends. She wasn't much different from all the other retirees in this town. Her grandma would have a field day retelling the incident at the senior center.

It took the police twenty minutes to respond to the call, pulling up behind Frank's Subaru. Officer Hopper glowered at them when she got out of the police cruiser. "I should have known the call would come from the Dynamic Duo. Who got kidnapped this time?"

"No one did, but we found a human rib bone," Po Po said, ignoring Officer Hopper's confrontational tone. "Sandra Rankin identified it. She used to be a nurse."

Officer Hopper glanced at each of them as if waiting for the punch line. "So just one bone?"

Raina swallowed the tang of bile in her mouth. "An entire rib cage." She turned away when Frank led Officer Hopper toward the rest of the bones in the middle of the field. It seemed Po Po's séance did call forth a ghost, but the message was lost in translation as far as she was concerned. Did Arthur Westchester come out to dig up the dead or bury it?

RAINA SPENT Sunday playing with her niece and making lemon drop brownie bars for the bake sale at the Trunk-or-Treat. Her grandma had requested something special, and she figured most people wouldn't think to mix tangy lemon with sweet chocolate.

After putting Lila and Po Po down for nap time, Raina cleaned up and strolled to the Venus Cafe to get takeout. She wasn't in the mood to make dinner, and the cafe would have the latest gossip on the murder investigation. It was too bad the police couldn't have a wiretap on the place because they would solve most of the crime in this town by listening in on these conversations.

The short walk in the late afternoon was perfect. The leaves crackled under Raina's shoes, and the crisp autumn air cleared her head. The general hubbub of conversation and coffee aroma drifting out of the cafe to the sidewalk soothed her nerves. Eliminating the Rankins should fill her with a sense of accomplishment, but instead, it opened another can of worms...or bones.

Arthur Westchester had looked for them, and someone didn't want him to find them. Why else would a man like Arthur purchase a new rake? Though a shovel would have probably done a better job, not that he would know. He wasn't a man who worked with his hands for a living.

Her grandma and her cronies stumbled on the bones by accident, so at least Raina didn't have to worry about the killer going after them. Maybe she should backtrack and figure out who owned the old pumpkin patch before Arthur had purchased it for development. Mostly she was afraid what Detective Sokol would do with the information without the chief or Matthew around to rein him in.

As Raina reached for the doorknob, a cell phone rang. She glanced around, not recognizing the ring tone. There was no one behind her. The phone rang again. It came from her purse. Right, the cell phone from her grandma. Talk about a bimbo moment. She stepped aside on the porch, almost bouncing in her haste. Finally! A lead on the kidnapper.

"Hello?" Her voice came out slightly breathless.

"Are you still looking for your nephew?" said the voice over the phone. He sounded gruff like someone trying to deepen his voice.

"Yes, but he's not my nephew. I'm holding onto this phone for my grandma. He's her nephew," Raina said. Did she overdo it with the explanation? "Do you know where he is? Everyone in the family is worried about him."

"What's his name?" the voice asked.

Raina hesitated. The caller must know the kidnapper, but not well enough to ignore the flyer and the lure of the reward money. "Is this a prank?" she asked, stalling.

"I want to make sure you know the man on the flyer. I don't want to be responsible if this turns out to be a domestic abuse situation."

Raina burst out laughing. "He's a big, brawny guy who could snap me like a twig. And you're afraid I'll beat him up with a frying pan?"

Silence.

Raina could sense the caller mulling over her words. "Look, call me back if you're still interested in the reward."

She held her breath, hoping he would take the hint. If the thought of losing the reward money didn't encourage the caller to talk, then anything she said wouldn't matter.

"Wait!" The caller's voice squeaked. "I didn't say—"

"Where is he?"

"I can't tell you over the phone. How will I get the reward money?" the voice croaked at the end. He sounded like a teenager whose voice hadn't stopped changing yet.

Raina sighed. Why were things never easy? "Where and when do you want to meet? Tonight?"

"I...uh, I'm busy in the evenings."

Uh-huh. His parents probably didn't let him leave the house after dark. "How about tomorrow morning?"

"Can't. I have class."

"Are you a college student?" Raina asked. She doubted he was old enough to drive. "Maybe we can meet on campus? I have class in the morning too."

"Tuesday at four o'clock," the caller said. "At the Pancake House."

"Okay," Raina said, dragging out the word. Her grandma would love this espionage business. "So how would we recognize each other? What is your name?"

"No names," the caller said. "What color is your scarf?"

"I don't have a scarf, but I have an orange beanie."

"I will look for you."

"But—"

He hung up.

Raina glanced at the display on the prepaid phone. There was no number on caller ID. The caller sounded more like a kid than an adult. She hoped she wouldn't have to answer to his parents.

As she tucked the phone back into her purse, her other cell phone rang. It was Detective Sokol. She glanced at the time. Almost five o'clock. Her grandma and Lila would be awake by now. Should she let the call go to voicemail? But he might have information on the bones they had found at the pumpkin patch.

Raina glanced longingly through the window at the warm glowing fireplace inside the café and hit the talk button. "Hello?"

"Miss Sun, are you busy?" the detective said jovially. He sounded too pleased with himself.

"I can talk, but make it quick."

"We found more human bones in the field."

Raina's eyes widened. A mass grave? This was even worse than a random rib cage. Something like this would hold up the mall construction indefinitely. Was this why Arthur was trying to dig it up without witnesses? How did he even suspect there might be a problem with the site?

"How many victims did you find?" she asked.

"I don't know yet, but we have a serial murderer hiding among us." There was a hint of triumph in his voice. Bringing in a serial murderer would guarantee his promotion.

The hair on the back of Raina's neck stiffened, and she glanced around in the dusk. She didn't see anyone. Probably just nerves and too many shadows beyond the faint porch light and streetlights.

"How do you know it's a serial murderer? There might be another explanation for this," Raina asked, wincing at the hitch in her voice.

It would be too soon for the county's forensic team to make this determination. And since it was a weekend, the evidence wouldn't have made it to the county lab yet.

"My experience tells me we have a serial murderer. Don't worry, Miss Sun, I will do everything in my power to protect the people in this town." And with this, he hung up on her.

Raina shook her head at the phone. What the heck? With Halloween around the corner, a rumor like this could start a mass panic. Matthew needed to hear about this. She dialed his cell phone, and it went straight to voicemail. She hung up and tried again.

"Seriously?" she said out loud. What was the point of having a cell phone when she couldn't get in touch with someone when she needed it?

"What is this about a serial murderer in town?" a deep baritone voice asked.

Raina jumped, dropping her phone. It slid through the railings.

Crack!

Another dead phone. Yep, right on time. It disappeared into the shrubbery.

She spun around, and the menacing shadow of a big man came at her with his hands raised.

13

AN USUAL PARTNERSHIP

As Robert Spillman stepped into the porch light, Raina swallowed the scream in her throat. It came out in a gasp like she just came out of the water in a pool.

Her heart battered rapidly against her chest, and her blood roared in her ears. This rapid reversal from a threat to civilized exchange left her dizzy. She sagged against the railing on the porch.

Robert's weary brown eyes watched her, his square face quizzical like he was trying to figure her out. "If you're lucky, the drop only cracked the screen. I hope you have insurance."

Raina nodded, still trying to calm her racing pulse. Where did he come from? And how much did he hear?

"What's this about a serial murderer and multiple victims?" he asked again.

"What are you talking about?" Raina hoped she sounded confused.

"I didn't mean to eavesdrop, but I was coming in from the parking lot. I could hear you clearly. Who were you talking to? Toni Moody?"

She gave him her sweetest smile. "Most people would make more noise to politely let others know they are listening in on a private conversation."

"My mama always said I was light on my feet for such a big guy." Robert patted his paunch. "Were you talking about the bodies they discovered at the old pumpkin patch?"

"What...what bodies?" she asked through numb lips. It was bad enough she was linked to the only private investigator in town; she didn't want to be linked to the discovery of a mass grave too.

"You haven't heard?" He gestured at the inside of the café. "I'll bet you dinner that's what everyone in there's talking about." His tone was flippant, but there was an undercurrent of tension in it.

She wasn't taking him up on the offer. "I'm not interested in gossip. Excuse me. I have to get my phone."

He raised an eyebrow. "Right, from the girl who snooped at my receptionist's desk?"

"I was looking—"

"I dropped the check for Arthur's outstanding invoice in the mail this morning. Call the office if you don't get it," he said.

"Thank you," Raina said, backing away from him. He was too accommodating. What did he want from her? "I have to get my phone."

"The bodies were found at the old pumpkin patch, you know. So bye-bye mall," he said conversationally. "Who do you think alerted the police? Those neighbors? The Rankins?"

"You would have to ask them." *Please don't.* She gripped the railings and inched her way down the three steps to the sidewalk. "I have to get my phone."

"Can you see in the dark?" He held up his cell phone and turned on the light, shining it on her face. "You can use my phone as a flashlight."

Raina held out her hand to block the light. "No, thanks. I can manage."

Robert shrugged and went inside the café. As the door swung closed, Raina let out a sigh of relief. She didn't know what came over her.

This was the perfect opportunity to grill him about the mall and his affair with Mia. Instead, she fumbled like he had all the leverage in the conversation.

There were plenty of people inside the café, though she doubted if they would notice or hear a scuffle outside at this time of day. In her previous investigations, she had investigated in the shadows, hiding from the murderer. The suspects never knew her connection to the case until the end.

But her connection to Moody Investigation put her out in the open and left her vulnerable and apprehensive. She didn't know who the murderer might be, and she couldn't guard against all the suspects. How did a private investigator deal with this?

Raina walked around the steps until she was close

to the area where her phone took a flying leap from her hand. She hunched down, shining the prepaid phone's light at the shrubbery underneath the porch. Nothing. She dialed her phone number, then remembered she had turned off the ringtone. She must have a cell phone curse. Maybe it was time to go retro and get a brick for a phone.

She tucked the prepaid phone back into her purse. She would have to come back in the morning to look again. Maybe after her morning run. Eventually, she would have to apologize to Brenda for recommending Eden to work at the Venus Cafe. It might as well be tomorrow.

A car squealed around a corner, and headlights shone into her face. She squinted, holding a hand to block the light. If the car were to jump the curb, she would become a pancake.

Raina lurched to the right, throwing herself into the shrubbery, and rolled like an untrained stunt double. She stopped at the edge of the gravel parking lot. Her knees and elbows stung from multiple scratches.

A car door opened and slammed shut, footsteps stomped up the wooden stairs, and the cafe door opened and closed. The driver hadn't even noticed Raina on the ground. She got up slowly. Her shaking hand pushed the curly black hair off her face. She didn't want to go inside the cafe. One look at her would start a rumor there was a serial rapist on the loose.

She hobbled up to the cafe, peering from window

to window. There! At the table on the left side of the fireplace sat Robert and the kidnapper.

As Raina crept around the side of the cafe, she couldn't help but wonder how the patrons would react if she were caught. It could embarrass Matthew, especially if he ended up being chief someday. She wished she could be more like her grandma, embracing eccentricity, so she didn't have to worry about ruining his career. But even her grandma was a dutiful wife while her husband was building his shipping empire.

The pungent trash container hit her before she could make out its dark shape huddled next to the building. Oh great. If she wanted to get close enough to the window to eavesdrop on Robert and the kidnapper, she would need to huddle next to the trash container. And since pickup day was tomorrow morning, the container held an entire week of moldy and putrid garbage from the restaurant.

With the vegetation and trees in the side yard, the moonlight was more of a hindrance than a help, casting deep shadows and distorting the ground elevation. She held her hands in front of her like an actress pretending to be a blind person, inching along on the gravel path. At the rate she was going, Robert and the kidnapper would be done with their conversation before she even got close enough to eavesdrop on them. Was it even worth the potential fall in the dark and assault on her nose to listen in?

Footsteps crunched on the gravel path behind her. Raina spun around, but couldn't make out who was there. A beam of light swept around like this person had every right to be here. Must be a restaurant worker.

Raina took a step backward until she was further underneath the canopy of the tree next to her. Her pulse raced. This was a bad idea. She should have gone home. Why didn't she put on her ninja outfit so she could blend in with the shadows?

"Rainy?" a familiar voice whispered. The faint outline of a woman appeared in front of her. What was her grandma doing here?

"Po Po," Raina whispered, stepping forward.

"Gaaah!" Po Po screamed, dropping her flashlight.

The window curtain flickered open, and Robert peered into the yard. The flashlight shone back at the house, highlighting the trash container. Robert squinted at the light.

Raina grabbed her grandma's hand and pulled her underneath the tree. "Shhh! They will hear us." She hoped Robert would think the flashlight was a land-scaping light.

Po Po clamped a hand over her mouth. Her breaths came out in audible puffs.

Raina could feel her grandma's racing pulse through the skin of her hand. If her grandma ended up with a heart attack...

Robert closed the window and disappeared from sight.

Raina picked up her grandma's flashlight, which turned out to be her cell phone. "What are you doing here? How did you know I was back here?"

Po Po patted her chest. "I got your note about picking up food, but it's been over an hour. I came by to make sure you were okay. And I saw you sneaking around the building. Actually, you weren't sneaking. You were limping like Frankenstein with your leg stuck out at a funny angle. It wasn't sexy."

Raina sighed. "Can you go inside to get the food? I'll wait for you outside. I'll tell you about my grand adventure on the way home."

They walked back to the front of the building, and her grandma went inside. She came out a few minutes later holding a large plastic bag.

"You're not going to believe this," Po Po said.

"The kidnapper is inside?" Raina said.

"Was this why you were sneaking around in the dark?"

"No, I was trying to be a ninja," Raina said, heading back toward the condo.

"Wait! Don't you want to hear their conversation?"

"Short of sitting next to them at the table, I don't see how this would be possible."

Po Po gave her a sly smile. She pulled out a small black box with dials like a radio receiver.

Raina's jaw dropped open. "No way! You have a wiretap on the restaurant?"

"Under the salt and pepper shakers." Po Po shrugged. "Why do you think I come here so often? It's not for the food." She turned the dials until a faint crackle came through.

"We can't listen to them here. What if someone sees us?" Raina whispered, looking around. No one was in sight.

As a car drove past, the white reflectors on her grandma's blackened orthopedic shoes lit up in the darkness.

"We can't go too far away, or we won't have a signal," Po Po said.

"Let's go back to the trash container."

"No, thanks. That smell will get in my hair."

"How about the parking lot?" Raina said. It was better than standing in front of the cafe under the porch light.

Po Po trotted toward the gravel parking lot, tuning her receiver.

"...idiot. I'm not buying the property..." the unfamiliar voice said. Might be the kidnapper.

"...Riviera family land...habitat..." Robert's deep baritone voice said.

"...dessert?" an unfamiliar female voice said.

"...full..." Robert said.

"...check when ready..." the unfamiliar female voice said.

"There's too much interference. We need to get closer," Po Po whispered.

"Let's see what we can pick up after the waitress leaves," Raina said.

"...Mia...interested..." Robert said.

"...sis...out..." the kidnapper said.

Silence.

Raina glanced behind them. Still empty. They would need to clear the parking lot before Robert came back for his car.

Po Po fiddled with the receiver.

Silence.

The area brightened, and Raina turned to see Robert standing by the café doorway. He faced away from the parking lot to speak to the kidnapper half a step behind him. Raina grabbed her grandma's arm and tugged her toward the café's van. They crouched down and waited. A couple of minutes later, a car engine came to life, and gravel crunched as Robert's car left the parking lot.

As they strolled back to the condo, Po Po said something about getting better equipment, but Raina tuned her out.

The dinner meeting between Robert and the kidnapper could only mean one thing. Robert, the kidnapper, and Mia knew each other and covered up the kidnapping. What Raina couldn't wrap her mind around was why? Why did the kidnapping occur in the first place? And why cover it up? Did she mistake a prank for something more nefarious? Or were the three of them accomplices in Arthur Westchester's murder?

14

THE BEGINNING OF THE END

Raina clutched her cell phone and pulled it from the shrubbery outside the Venus Café. She swiped an arm across her forehead, wiping off the sweat with her long sleeve shirt. She better get inside. Once her body cooled down from her morning jog, she would start shivering in her shorts. She sighed at the cracked screen and the missing battery cover. She should get a job with a cell phone allowance plan.

The café was transitioning from the early morning off-to-work crowd to the college-student-to-class crowd. Raina ordered her coffee and bagel with pumpkin spice cream cheese and went to a table next to the fireplace. She moved the window shade aside and glanced outside to the side yard. Even in the morning light, it was still in deep shade. Robert couldn't have seen her out there last night.

Brenda came over with the coffee and bagel on a

plate. "I have something to tell you, Rainy." She glanced around and lowered her voice. "I'm pregnant."

Raina broke into a huge grin, jumping up from the chair to hug her friend. "Oh, my gosh! I'm so happy for you. Sit down. You need to get off your feet."

Brenda blushed, beaming. "Shhh! It's still early days yet. I've had a few miscar—"

"No, this time is different. I can feel it. You'll need to take it easy because you're not resting after she's born." Raina frowned. Why did she think it would be a girl?

"I would have to dye my hair when"—she lowered her voice—"the baby goes to school."

"Why?"

"I'll be fifty."

"Forty-eight."

"Close enough. I wouldn't fit in with the younger moms."

Raina chuckled. She could see the scene clearly in her mind. Maybe Brenda should dye it pink like her grandma. "You'll do fine. How's Joe taking the news?"

The amusement left Brenda's face. "He's doing the whole stoic man thing, but I can tell he's scared of what another miscarriage would do to me and our marriage." She lowered her eyes, and a tear slid down her face.

Raina handed Brenda a napkin from the holder on the table. "How far along are you?"

Her friend wiped her eyes. "Almost eleven weeks and everything is still good."

"See! This time it's different. Tell Joe he has nothing to worry about. It'll be fine."

Brenda's smile wobbled. "I need your help, Rainy. I want more time off at the café. No, I need more time off." She gave Raina a pleading look. "And Eden quit."

"I'm sorry about Eden. I thought she'd changed."

"Well, here's your chance to make it up to me."

"There's my job at Moody Investigations. Toni will retire soon and sell the practice…"

"We'll work around your schedule. It'll just be for a couple of years at most."

"Do I get a cell phone allowance?"

Brenda chuckled. "No. That would cost me a small fortune."

"What are the perks?"

"You can have all the coffee you want."

"Man, you drive a hard bargain. I'm only doing this part-time." As soon as the words left her mouth, Raina realized she had become a cupcake-baking amateur sleuth. Her ancestors had turned her life into a cliché.

"Excellent! By the way, what do you think the press conference is about?"

"What are you talking about?" Raina said, reaching for her coffee.

"Oh, I thought you would know. The police are holding a press conference about the mass grave at the old pumpkin patch. Didn't you help discover it?"

"Who said I discovered it?"

"Detective Sokol. He gave you all the credit for calling the police. Then he said we need more Good

Samaritans like you in this town." Brenda frowned. "I don't like this. There's an active murder investigation going on, and he turned the target on you. Makes me feel like he's using you as bait."

Raina choked on her coffee, and Brenda thumped on her back. When her coughs subsided, Raina croaked, "He'll cause a panic in this town."

BRENDA WENT BACK TO CUSTOMERS, and Raina finished her breakfast. She called Matthew again, but it went straight to voicemail again. He was probably in his training class. She left a message about the press conference this afternoon.

Raina trotted back to her apartment, texting her grandma on the way.

WHEN ARE THE POLICE HOLDING THEIR PRESS CONFERENCE THIS AFTERNOON? ALSO NEED JOANNA HOPPER'S PHONE NUMBER. THANKS AND LOVE YOU.

Her grandma replied back.

ON IT, SHERLOCK.

As she showered and changed, Raina wondered if she should go to class. With only a few hours left until the press conference, she needed help if she were to stop Detective Sokol from causing widespread panic.

Driving around town hoping to run into Officer Hopper's police cruiser could be a waste of time.

But her professor would assign teams for the class project this afternoon, and she risked being partnered with a lazy classmate if she didn't show up.

Raina glanced at the gilded koi clock above her TV. There wasn't enough time for everything. She'd have to skip class. Failing class meant paying for another semester, but failing Matthew wasn't an option.

Her phone dinged on the way out the door. It was a message from Po Po.

Cassie wants to extend her stay. We got the monkey for a few more days. Still checking on the other stuff.

She put the prepaid phone back into her purse. *Please let things work out between Cassie and Benson*, she thought.

Raina pulled into the parking lot at the police station. There was no point in waiting for her grandma to get back to her.

Donna, the desk clerk, was on the phone when Raina walked in. "Yes, we're still holding the press conference. Two o'clock on the lawn outside the station."

Raina turned her back, pretending to look at the flyers on the community bulletin board. If Donna cared about privacy, she wouldn't have taken the call where anyone could listen in.

"While the Chief and his senior staff are in training, Detective Sokol is acting chief and authorized to give this press conference." Donna hung up the phone.

Raina turned around and gave the clerk a bright smile. "Hi, Donna."

Donna was a plump, pleasant brunette with flashing blue eyes. She didn't have a malicious bone in her body, but she loved to hear herself talk. Probably because she often spent the day alone at the front counter.

"Hi, Rainy. Are you making something for the Trunk-or-Treat?" Donna asked.

Raina nodded. "The Posse Club is selling them. Lemon chocolate brownie bars."

Donna's eyes lit up. She also happened to have a sweet tooth.

"I'll tell my grandma to save one for you," Raina said, winking. "It'll be on the house."

"Trying to bribe me with food again, huh?"

"Yeah. Is it working?"

"What do you need?" Donna said.

"I'm looking for Officer Hopper. Do you know where I can find her? Even better, can I have her cell phone number?"

"No, on the cell phone, but I can call her on the radio to see where she's at."

Donna turned away from Raina to speak in the walkie-talkie. Raina couldn't hear a word of the exchange. Apparently, the clerk could be discreet when she needed to be. A few minutes later she turned back to Raina.

"Officer Hopper is at Moody Investigation. She'll be there for a few more minutes," Donna said.

Raina's heart sank. The only reason Officer Hopper would speak with her boss would be to complain about Raina's involvement in the murder investigation. What was her problem? "Did she say why she is there?"

Donna shook her head. "Sorry, I didn't ask."

Raina thanked the clerk and trotted back to her car. Sure, Officer Hopper didn't want Raina sticking her nose into the murder case, but she wasn't in charge. The lead detective and acting police chief had asked her to help him out.

Ten minutes later, she pulled up next to the police cruiser in the parking lot. When she strolled into Moody Investigation, Toni's office door was closed. Officer Hopper must have a long list of complaints.

Raina pulled her paycheck from the filing cabinet and tucked it into her purse. She returned to her desk and fired up the computer. As she waited, she glanced at the open cases in the Inbox tray—a potential fraudulent workers compensation claim and a surveillance job for a divorce case. How could she focus on ordinary cases when there was a murder occupying her thoughts?

When the computer finished booting, she typed Robert Spillman Junior into the database for public records on the computer and hit enter. The hourglass icon twirled for several seconds. Sure enough, there was a court record for him.

Raina scanned the information. Embezzlement? She tapped the desk with her fingers. After spending a year in the slammer, where did Bobby get the funds to open an insurance agency? It didn't sound like his father helped him out. Did he have a silent partner?

She didn't like the idea of an unknown player. Surely, Bobby and this unknown silent partner—if there was one—had nothing to do with Arthur Westchester's death? What would be the link? Bobby's obsession with Mia?

She typed in the assessor's parcel number for the old pumpkin patch. The computer hourglass twirled and returned a list of property owner names: Westchester Development, LLC, Riviera Family Trust, Jose Ortega, and nothing before the 1900s. It looked like the Westchester Development had acquired the property during the recent housing bust. She wondered if the Rivieras and Ortegas were different branches of the same family.

The office door clicked open, and Raina grabbed the worker's compensation file. She lifted her gaze to find both Toni Moody and Officer Hopper glaring at her.

15

A SOUR DISAPPOINTMENT

The sparks from Officer Hopper's flinty eyes were nothing new. She stalked out of the office, her blonde hair swaying behind her back like a satisfied cat.

Raina wanted to run after her—she wasn't sure if it was to punch her or plead with her to help stop the press conference—but the look in her boss's eyes stopped her.

While Toni had always been a formidable woman, her dark brown eyes and rotund build had radiated kindness that reminded Raina of Precious Ramotswe from the *No. 1 Ladies Detective Agency*. Now her boss's brows were furrowed and the lips tightly pressed. Even her silver braid seemed taut with tension. She marched out of the office and went to pour a cup of coffee from the carafe in the corner by the microwave and mini refrigerator. The temperature in the office dropped by several degrees.

Raina returned her gaze to the computer screen. If she didn't make eye contact, maybe her boss would return to her office. She entered the person's name into an online background check database. It was part of her job to enter the names into the various databases to see if anything unusual popped up. This prep work could be rather tedious, but was perfect for today.

Toni cleared her throat, and Raina cringed inwardly but glanced up with a smile.

"Officer Hopper is threatening to arrest us for obstructing justice," Toni said. "Apparently, we're harassing witnesses and contaminating evidence in our investigation of Arthur Westchester's death." She raised an eyebrow. "I told her there must be a mistake because we're not on the case."

Raina squirmed in her chair, averting her eyes. She should come clean, but what if Toni fired her for abusing her connection with Moody Investigation to get witnesses to talk to her?

Silence.

Toni started tapping her foot.

Delay would only make matters worse for Raina. As she opened her mouth, her purse started vibrating, and the *Gangnam Style* song filled the office. Raina flushed, grabbing for the prepaid phone to turn off the ring tone. Her grandma must have programmed her number to play this song.

Toni's face softened as if she was trying to hold back laughter. "You were saying?"

"Uh...I ran into Officer Hopper a couple of times while chatting with some people," Raina said.

"I figured as much. A private investigator has no jurisdiction in a homicide. In this profession, you stay in the police's good graces."

"Aren't you even a teeny bit curious what triggered the kidnapping and the death?"

"I can't afford to be."

Raina blinked, digesting Toni's words. There were all kinds of expenses for a small business owner, but it still...sucked.

Toni must have guessed Raina's thoughts by the expression racing across her face. "I was idealistic once, but age and a mortgage have a way of knocking it out of you. I'm fifty-five years old, and I would like to retire before I'm sixty. I can't indulge in curiosity anymore."

"We found a mass grave at the old pumpkin patch."

"Tell me what you've learned so far."

Raina told Toni everything she knew, starting with the affair between Mia Westchester and Robert Spillman, Bobby's obsession with Mia, and the conversation between Robert and the kidnapper the evening before. "And later this afternoon there will be rumors a serial killer is on the loose if I don't stop the press conference."

Toni studied Raina for a long moment and finally nodded. "Maybe you should take a few days off to go scratch this itch. I don't want to link Moody Investigation to this case."

Raina considered her words and spoke carefully. "When does justice take second place to a mortgage?"

"When you have things to lose. If you keep this romanticized notion that you'll save the police or the citizens of this town, this job isn't for you. I deal with domestic issues and small crimes. Maybe other detectives have more exciting cases, but I doubt it."

Raina nodded, not in agreement but to acknowledge Toni's experience. There wasn't much she could say to change her boss's mind. Either she dropped the case, or she'd take a short leave of absence. She was already too invested to back out, and Matthew was counting on her. But if she continued investigating, and the case dragged out, Toni might replace Raina with someone else.

Losing another job would bother Raina, but not as much as losing the opportunity to get field experience for her PI license. She was caught between two boulders, and she didn't like the squeeze.

Toni sipped her coffee, calmly watching Raina. As if taking pity on Raina, she asked, "Were you able to collect on Arthur Westchester's outstanding invoice?"

"His business partner said the check is in the mail already."

"Thanks," Toni said. She hesitated and sipped her coffee again, probably reconsidering what she was about to say. "Have a good week. Hopefully, I will see you next week after you scratch this itch."

"I hope it will be sooner."

"For your sake, me too. Good luck."

Raina bid her boss goodbye. When she got back to her car, she checked the voicemail from her grandma. It said the press conference was at two o'clock and that she would meet Raina there.

Right now Raina wanted nothing to do with the press conference. She wanted to crawl in bed with her best buds, Ben and Jerry. The two of them always knew how to show her a good time.

She tightened her grip on the steering wheel. Tears formed in the back of her eyes, and she blinked rapidly, hoping they would go away. She didn't blame Toni one bit for her reaction—she even understood why—but she was disappointed.

She had thought, when the chips were down, Toni would offer her experience and insight on the Westchester case—to be Raina's secret weapon. This was her problem, not Toni's. She had projected a passion for justice onto her boss that didn't exist.

The prepaid cell phone dinged. The text message was from her grandma.

WILL SAVE YOU A SEAT.

Raina wiped her face with the back of her hand and started the engine. There was no time to wallow in her disappointment. Toni was who she was—a practical businesswoman. Private investigation was a means to a paycheck. But unlike Toni, Raina had another job at the café. She didn't need to work for this particular paycheck. Although, she hoped it wouldn't come down to this.

RAINA CIRCLED the police station twice but still couldn't find a parking spot. She ended up parking three blocks away. As she trotted back, people came out of shops and homes to join her. The chairs on the lawn were already taken, but she saw her grandma and her cronies in the front row. The speculations and rumors were well under way, creating a buzz that droned like a beehive. The press conference was turning out to be an event.

She scanned the crowd looking for Officer Hopper or Detective Sokol. She didn't expect to see him. Undoubtedly, he would mount the raised platform late to increase anticipation from the town folk. This could be the highlight of his career.

Raina edged around the crowd and went into the station. The whirling overhead fan and dim lights were the only sign of activity inside. Donna wasn't at the front counter, and the sea of desks in the bullpen was also empty. She rang the bell on the counter, not expecting anyone to come out. It must be all hands on deck to handle the crowd outside.

No one showed up.

Raina checked the prepaid phone. No messages from Matthew. What was he doing? Didn't he get any of her messages? She called him again. As the phone rang, she hit the bell on the front counter again.

Officer Hopper stepped through the archway on the far wall. She hesitated when she caught sight of Raina and sauntered to the front counter at a leisurely pace. "No questions until later."

Raina glanced behind her to make sure they were alone but lowered her voice anyway. "Is Detective Sokol really going to announce a serial killer? We both know there's no evidence of this."

Officer Hopper's eyes became guarded. "He's the acting chief."

"But he's wrong, and this will cause widespread panic."

"He's the acting chief."

"Is this all you have to say?"

"He's the acting—"

"Yes, we have already established this. Why aren't you doing anything to stop—" Raina cut herself off, frowning at the policewoman. Surely Officer Hopper wouldn't put personal gain above the safety of the town. "You...you want him to make this announcement."

"If Detective Sokol is mistaken, he'll have to answer to the chief," Officer Hopper said. Her tone was flat.

Raina blinked. Was there a hint of satisfaction in her voice?

Officer Hopper glanced at her watch. "Besides, I'm not authorized to stop him."

Raina watched Officer Hopper leave the building to

join the rest of the town. She sagged against the counter. Now what? She couldn't run outside and knock over the podium. The police would probably arrest her for disorderly conduct.

She had failed Matthew and probably lost her internship at Moody Investigation in one fell swoop. She covered her face with her hands and sank to her knees, overwhelmed and exhausted. Why would Officer Hopper risk the police department like this? She had to know Detective Sokol made the wrong call. She had to.

Raina stared at the privacy glass on the front door of the station. Blurred shapes moved against the gray sky. Loud feedback from a speaker startled her, and she clasped her hands on her ears. The squawk faded, and Donna came onto the microphone to introduce Detective Sokol. Even through the heavy set of double doors, Raina could hear the press conference.

A male voice cleared his throat. "I hate to be the bringer of bad news..."

Raina shook her head. There was nothing she could do to fix this mess. Nothing. She got up with shaking legs to go home. She would deal with the fallout after meeting with the informant in the morning. Maybe the identity of the kidnapper would shed a light on the murder investigation and mass grave. The rest of Detective Sokol's speech would only make things murkier, and her grandma could fill her in on the highlights later.

16

A NEW RECRUIT

The next afternoon, Raina had to rope Frank Small into babysitting Lila again. With no grandchild of his own, her grandma's friend was more than happy to have a little one to build Legos with him at the senior center. Raina and Po Po kissed the child goodbye and left to meet the informant at the Pancake House.

Raina took off her jacket but kept the orange beanie on. She slid into the booth next to the window. Now she could see anyone coming toward the restaurant.

Po Po tossed off her red velvet tuxedo jacket. Her gold medallion glinted against the weak afternoon sun. "So why are we meeting this informant at the Pancake House?"

"I don't know. The person on the phone said he wanted to meet here. I didn't want to argue with him,"

Raina said, glancing down at her menu. "Besides, I want pumpkin pancakes."

They placed their orders with the server. Raina glanced at the display on the prepaid phone. The kid was already late. She scratched her head underneath the orange beanie. He better show soon, or she would melt into a puddle from the heat in the restaurant.

"What happened to your phone?" Po Po asked.

"What makes you think anything happened to my phone?" Raina said.

Po Po smirked. "Broke your phone again, huh?"

Raina pressed her lips together and ignored her grandma's comment. "What's up with the costume?"

"I want to get into character. I got fifty pounds of candy for the Club Posse booth." Po Po sat up straighter, tipping her chin. "We are so beating Smelly Tally, both for the popular booth and performance."

"Po Po, you shouldn't be calling people names. How—"

Her grandma held up a hand to stop Raina. "I'm too old for a lecture. I could die tomorrow. If I want to call my nemesis a name, I've earned the right."

Raina held up both hands, palms out. "All right. Smelly Tally it is. How did the town react to the serial killer news?"

Po Po's face darkened. "The man is a menace. If I were the chief, I would fire him."

"Remember the twin babies?" Raina said. "They need to eat."

"Fine. I would demote him to dog catcher."

"So people dismissed his news?"

Po Po shook her head. "They believe it all right. Smelly Tally is locking herself in her unit until they find the serial killer. Too bad she plans to come out for the Trunk-or-Treat though."

With the town up in arms over the serial killer, it would be even more difficult to get answers about Arthur Westchester's death. The cynical part of Raina wondered if Detective Sokol announced the serial killer news to muddy things up for Matthew when he got back. After all, he could blame his lack of experience with homicide to back out of the investigation.

"I haven't been able to get in touch with Matthew the last couple of days," Raina said.

Po Po rolled her eyes. "Just because you're engaged doesn't mean the two of you have to be joined at the hip. He's probably overwhelmed by what he's learning. Whether he likes it or not, he'll be our next police chief."

Raina gave her grandma a suspicious look. "Do you know something I don't know?"

"I'm your elder. Of course, I know more than you. It's a perk of getting old."

Raina smooshed her face with her hands. "You mean old like this?"

Po Po laughed and swatted her arm. "You're not Lila. No old jokes from you."

Raina chuckled. "Fine." She told Po Po her theory that Arthur Westchester might have been looking for evidence of the mass grave before his death. "I think we need to have another chat with Mia Westchester."

"How will we get past the big dog and the gun? Your cookies and charm won't cut it, Rainy."

"I'll have to resort to arm twisting. She wouldn't like the public to know about her affair with Robert Spillman." Raina's voice was flat. She didn't like playing hardball, but sometimes it was the only way to get answers.

Through the window, she caught sight of a glum teenager pushing a bike with a flat tire toward the restaurant. As he locked his bike, she signaled to her grandma. "He's here."

Po Po glanced around. "Where?"

"Wait for it."

The teenager strolled through the door, glancing around the restaurant. He looked like he was of Middle Eastern descent and stood about five nine. His thick black hair fell into a flop around his large brown eyes. His shirt was too loose, his pants too baggy, and they hung three inches too low, exposing a swath of plaid flannel boxers. Either the gold chain around his neck was too heavy for him, or he wasn't used to his height yet because he walked with a stoop.

When he glanced in their direction, Raina grabbed her orange beanie and waved it above her head. His eyes widened, and he slid into the booth next to Raina, giving her the once-over and a cheeky grin. "Sup, babe. My name is T-Dawg."

Raina bit the inside of her cheek to stop the

laughter threatening to burst out. He must think he was a smooth operator.

Po Po cleared her throat, and T-Dawg glanced across the booth. He flushed, and when he swallowed, his Adam's apple bobbed. Her grandma tipped her chin at the teen. "You here for the reward?"

"You got the money?" T-Dawg asked. He rested one arm behind the booth, so his fingers touched the tips of Raina's hair.

She shifted and jammed her elbow against his hand, pinning his fingers to the booth. "Oops, sorry about that, T-Dawg."

He squeaked and jerked his hand back to his side. "No worries, old thang. We can work it out later."

Raina rolled her eyes at her grandma. Between Po Po's K-pop outfit and the teen's rapper bling, Raina decided to let the two of them hash it out. They both seemed to enjoy their roles immensely.

"So where's my nephew?" Po Po asked, narrowing her eyes at the teen.

"So where's my money?" the teen asked.

"I'm not showing you the money until I get the information I need."

"Well, I'm not giving you any information till I get my money."

Raina held up her hands for a timeout. She addressed T-Dawg. "We're not showing you the money until we check out your lead. You'll have to trust we will give you the money."

T-Dawg squinted his eyes at the two of them. "Half now, half—"

The server slid platters in front of Raina and Po Po. She grabbed her notepad and glanced at the teen. "You want anything, hon?"

T-Dawg's eyes gleamed as he stared at the food. He licked his lips and glanced at Po Po but addressed the server. "I'll have one of each." He gestured at the platters in front of them.

The server took down his order and left. Po Po slid her plate across the table to T-Dawg. "Why don't you start first? I can wait."

The teen rubbed his hands together. "Don't mind if I do. Thank you."

T-Dawg tucked into the food, inhaling the ham, bacon, and sausage next to the sunny-side up eggs. He had finished half the platter by the time the server returned with his order. She slid the platters on the table and left.

Raina lost her appetite watching him eat. A pig gorging before the slaughter would have been a better sight. "When was the last time you ate?"

T-Dawg swallowed the full bite in his mouth, pausing for a millisecond. "Lunch. I only had a turkey sandwich."

"I used to eat like you," Po Po said. "Now I can barely have a slice of bacon without gassing the place out."

T-Dawg paused with his fork suspended like he was waiting for the other part of the joke. Po Po poured syrup over her pumpkin pancakes until a moat surrounded it, ignoring his reaction. He shrugged and moved on to the second platter.

For the next few minutes, Po Po and the teen ate while Raina pushed her pancakes around the plate. When T-Dawg pushed his plate aside and belched, Raina asked, "Now that you have eaten your fill, are you ready to talk?"

T-Dawg rubbed his stomach. "So the man is your nephew?" He addressed Po Po, and his voice dripped with doubt.

"Actually, I don't know him," Po Po said. "He side-swiped a car and took off. I want him to pay for it."

T-Dawg frowned. "Are you sure Mateo hit your car? He's nutso about the environment, but he doesn't seem like the type to hit your car and take off."

"If it's not him, how was I able to describe him to the sketch artist?" Po Po asked, ignoring his comment about her car.

As T-Dawg mulled over Po Po's words, the server approached them.

"Can I get you anything else?" the server asked.

Raina shook her head. "Just the bill please."

After the server left, T-Dawg slapped his hands on the table. "I'll help you, but I want the money upfront. I need another five hundred to get this car they're selling at Pete's Pick-n-Pull. He's holding it for me until tomorrow." His large brown eyes pleaded with them.

"How do you even know Mateo?" Po Po asked, her

voice brisk. She wanted to convey she wasn't fooled, but Raina could see her grandma's gears spinning.

"We live in the same apartment complex. He's studying environmental science at the university. Always talking about how development will get rid of all the farmland in the region," T-Dawg said, shrugging. "I don't understand half the stuff he complains about. My mom and I worry about real stuff like making the rent."

"What's your real name?" Po Po asked.

T-Dawg looked down, staring at the table. "Ahanu Ahmet."

Po Po whipped out her cell phone and dialed someone's number. "I'll be right back." She went outside.

Through the storefront windows, Raina saw her grandma chatting on the phone. She suspected her grandma called Pete to verify Ahanu's story. "What else do you know about Mateo?"

The teen shrugged, still staring at the table. "He has a smoking hot sister. It's too bad she's so old though."

"What's old? Forties?"

He glanced up, frowning. "Maybe ten years older than you."

Raina wiped her mouth with a napkin to cover her smile. She'd asked for it. So Mateo's sister was probably in her late thirties. "Anything else? What's his last name?"

Ahanu opened his mouth. "Riv—"

"The car is a piece of junk. Needs new tires and a new engine," Po Po said, sliding back into the booth.

Raina gave Po Po a sideways glance. Her grandma was up to something.

"I can rebuild the engine," Ahanu said. "I'm good with mechanical stuff. And I can get another thousand miles or so on the tires. By then, I would save enough money to replace them."

Po Po's eyes went half-mast. "Is that right?" She waited half a second. "I bought the car."

The teen jumped up from his seat. "Wha—"

Po Po held up her hand. "It's yours, but I have a few conditions."

Ahanu's brows narrowed, and his lower lip jutted out, but he sat back down. "What conditions?"

"We can talk later," Po Po said mysteriously.

Raina glanced at the table to hide her smile. She could see her grandma planned to take this kid under her wing.

"My mom takes the bus at five in the morning to get to work," Ahanu said. "She can sleep in longer if I drive her." His voice cracked, and he averted his gaze. His hands curled into fists on his lap.

"I plan to be fair if you're straight with me." Po Po's voice softened. "I want you to meet some friends of mine."

Ahanu's eyes wide. "Friends?"

"They're good students at the high school, so your mom has nothing to worry about. But they make things...for me."

Ahanu shot Raina a glance. She grinned and twirled a finger around her head. "Craaa-zee," she mouthed.

"Stop it, Rainy," Po Po said, laughing. She addressed Ahanu, "I sponsor the Science Ninjas. Maybe you heard of them?"

"I thought that secret club was a fake. Are you telling me it's real?" Ahanu's eyes glittered with excitement.

Po Po raised an eyebrow and put a finger to her mouth. "Shhh!"

Raina cleared her throat. Time to redirect the conversation back to Mateo the kidnapper. "What is Mateo's last name?"

Ahanu took half a heartbeat to reply like he was still in shock. "Riviera. His sister's name is Mia."

Raina stiffened. Riviera? That was the last name of the previous owner for the old pumpkin patch. If the kidnapper was Mia Riviera Westchester's younger brother, no wonder she pretended as if nothing happened.

17

ANOTHER NUTSO

While Po Po and Ahanu hashed out their arrangement, Raina looked up the address for Mateo's apartment. It was on the east side of the railroad tracks, which was the seedier part of town. Lousy Larry's Burgers was considered the better part of that area. She needed to leave the neighborhood before it got dark. She could understand why the teen wanted the car to drive his mother in the morning. Ahanu thanked Po Po and left to fix the flat tire on his bike.

Half an hour later, Raina and Po Po watched the apartment complex over the dash of her car. Graffiti covered the two-story stucco apartment complex that had twelve units in a U-shape. The courtyard—she was being generous with the term—consisted of a square patch of dirt, weeds, and broken sprinkler heads. There was no on-site parking, but an abandoned car without tires guarded the entrance to the apartment.

"What do you think?" Po Po whispered.

Raina chewed her lower lip. "I don't know. We could get tetanus from using the handrail." The rusty metal handrail looked as if it would crumble under their hands.

"We can wait until it's darker to bust in." Mateo's unit was on the second floor, so there would be no creeping up to a window.

"I don't want to be here when it gets dark. Maybe we could call and get him to come outside," Raina said. The teen had given them Mateo's cell phone number.

"He wouldn't answer an unknown number."

They were silent for several minutes, contemplating their next move. What they needed was a police escort. Or weapons of mass destruction.

"We could call Officer Hopper to let her know we found the kidnapper," Raina said. "She might help us if it redeems her with the guys at the station."

"Good thinking," Po Po said, pulling out her phone. "I'll make the call."

Raina ignored her grandmother's side of the conversation. If they couldn't talk to Mateo, they should try to put the squeeze on his sister. How did Mia end up marrying Arthur Westchester? Did they fall in love over the sale of the Riviera land?

The family sold the land to Arthur in the recent housing bust probably because they needed the cash. If they were doing well financially, they would have held onto the land until the economy turned around.

What was the source of contention between Riviera

siblings? No matter what anyone else said, the kidnapping looked real to Raina. Mia must have agreed to something for Mateo to let her go. Was she an accomplice—however reluctantly—in her husband's death?

Po Po hung up and snapped her fingers in front of Raina's face. "Look alive, kid."

"Is Officer Hopper..." Raina trailed off. What was that sound?

"What—"

"Shhh! Do you hear that?"

Raina strained her ears. Nothing. She rolled down the car window. There! The faint wail of a police siren, growing louder as it approached their direction.

"Wow, that was fast," Po Po said.

Raina shook her head. "I don't think so. Someone must have called the police on us for loitering."

"In this neighborhood? Fat chance. Someone either died, or they're arresting a fugitive," Po Po said. Her eyes sparkled. "And we get a front row seat to all the action."

Three police cruisers pulled up with flashing lights and blaring sirens on either side of Raina's car, boxing her in. Her eyes widened. Five officers rushed out, three heading for the staircase and two going around back. Detective Sokol and Officer Hopper strolled past the Honda Accord and went to wait at the bottom of the staircase.

Po Po threw off her seatbelt and opened the car door. "Let's go see what's going on."

"We should wait in the car," Raina said.

Po Po slammed the door and practically skipped over to Detective Sokol and Officer Hopper. Raina turned off the engine and trotted after her grandma.

As she approached, she heard her grandma asking, "What's going on here? Are you arresting a fugitive?"

"Ma'am, I need you to get back into your car. You're obstructing the law," Detective Sokol said.

The officers pounded on the door upstairs. "Police! Open your door!"

Raina's eyes widened in surprise. The unit belonged to Mateo Riviera. Did this have to do with Arthur Westchester's death or the mass grave?

Detective Sokol glanced up, fingering the gun handle in the holster on his side. His eyes gleamed, reminding Raina of a religious fanatic. She shivered and turned away from him to find Officer Hopper watching her.

Raina grabbed her grandma's elbow and steered her toward the car. "We'll still have a front row seat."

Officer Hopper mimed a phone with her hand next to the side of her face. "Let's talk later," she mouthed.

Raina's eyes widened, but she nodded. Officer Hopper initiating a conversation? The world must be ending.

"Kick the door down!" Detective Sokol shouted.

"Open up! We have a warrant," the officer called out to Mateo.

Raina spun around and marched back over to the detective. "What are you doing? Do you have a warrant or just cause for invading someone's home? This could become a lawsuit for the department."

"Last time, Miss Sun, get out of here," he said through clenched teeth. "Or you can join Mateo Riviera in the same holding cell."

Raina backed away, palms up. She didn't care if the detective got himself fired, but he was creating a mess for somebody else to clean up...somebody like Matthew. She joined her grandmother in the car.

The police proceeded to kick in the door, and a woman screamed upstairs. Raina whipped out the prepaid cell phone and hit the camera app to film the police. Detective Sokol had gone bonkers.

The police dragged a handcuffed Hispanic man out of the apartment. He was shirtless and shoeless. He was in his early twenties with the build of someone who spent far too much time in the gym. But in the fading dusk and up close, Mateo Riviera looked vulnerable and young.

A blonde woman ran out of the apartment, clattering down the stairs in house slippers and clutching a robe. "Mateo, what's going on?"

Even though the woman's voice was shrill, it sounded vaguely familiar to Raina. She squinted, but couldn't make out her features with the exterior light behind her back.

Detective Sokol stuck out an arm to block her from getting closer. "Ma'am, he's wanted for questioning at the station. We'll release him once we're done with him."

The woman shoved at his arm. "I've never seen the cell phone before. It's not ours."

"Has anyone else been inside your home in the last week?"

"No, it's just the two of us. We don't usually invite people over," the woman said.

"Then can you explain how the cell phone got into your apartment?" Detective Sokol asked. Though Raina couldn't see his face, there was a smirk in his voice that she didn't like.

"I don't know. It doesn't belong to us," the woman said, wringing her hands.

Raina groaned in the car. The woman was giving away too much information. She should threaten to call a lawyer to get the detective to back down.

"Ma'am, I'm just doing my job," Detective Sokol said.

"Then find out who would want to frame my boyfriend. In this day and age, an anonymous tip is a sign of the real perpetrator," the woman said.

A police officer stuffed Mateo into the back of the cruiser, but he jerked out of his seat. "Call my sister," Mateo said. The police officer shoved him back into the vehicle.

The police piled into the other vehicles. As Detective Sokol walked by Raina's car, he reached in and plucked the prepaid cell phone out of her hand.

"Hey! What do you think you're doing?" Raina said.

Detective Sokol tapped on the screen and tossed the phone to Officer Hopper. "We're confiscating your phone. We suspect there's questionable material on it."

"You can't take my phone without a warrant," Raina said. She didn't know if this was true or not.

"My warrant allows me to take anything I suspect as evidence back to the station," Detective Sokol said. He turned and swaggered back to his vehicle. Officer Hopper trudged after him with a professionally blank expression.

Raina glowered at his back. "You wait until I tell Matthew about this!"

Detective Sokol paused in the process of getting into his vehicle. "That might not be a bad idea." He slammed the car door and gunned the engine.

Within a few minutes, Raina and her grandma were alone with the blonde woman crying by the staircase. Window curtains twitched, but no one came out. It was that kind of neighborhood.

Raina got out of the car to approach the blonde woman, making more noise than necessary so as not to startle her. "Excuse me, are you okay? Do you need any help?" The woman glanced up, and Raina gasped in surprise. "Cora?"

The woman sniffled and wiped the tears from her face. "Raina? What are you doing here?"

"I came to talk to Mateo Riviera." At the mention of her boyfriend's name, Cora's lower lip wobbled again. "I saw what happened," Raina continued. "What's going on? The detective is a loony bin. You have to be careful around him."

Raina knew she was taking advantage of the situation, but if she didn't press her advantage, she wouldn't be able to help anyone. From what she had overheard, it sounded like someone planted a cell phone into Mateo Riviera's apartment.

Cora shook her head. "I don't understand what's going on. The police are saying Mateo called Arthur Westchester to lure him out to the pumpkin patch. But I never saw the cell phone before."

Things clicked into place for Raina. The killer had set a trap for Mateo to be the scapegoat. Was this a move to buy time to get out of town? "Let me guess— an anonymous tip?"

Cora grabbed Raina's hand. "You have to help me. Mateo had no reason to kill Arthur Westchester. If Mateo hated his brother-in-law, he wouldn't have gotten me the job at Westchester Development."

"Then why did he kidnap his sister the day before Arthur's death? It looks suspicious."

"Mia sold the family farm to Arthur without consulting him. He was under age at the time, and it wasn't right for her to make this decision alone and not tell him about it."

"How could he not know? There's been a lot of talk about the mall."

"He was a teenager, and his father just died. You can't expect him to pay attention to the politics in town. When he found out, his sister wouldn't even talk to him about it. The only way he got her attention was by shoving her into a van."

"Why do you think Mia married Arthur?" Raina asked.

Cora shrugged. "I don't know. Maybe she loved him?" She got up from the staircase. "I need to call Mia. She needs to know what happened to Mateo and get him a lawyer." She took two steps up and paused. She turned slowly and asked, "Why do you need to talk to Mateo? Please don't tell me this has anything to do with an outstanding invoice."

Raina swallowed at the chill in Cora's voice. This could make or break their tenuous friendship. "I came to talk to him about Mia's kidnapping. She made me look foolish in front of my boss by saying she was at the spa. I want Mateo to support my story."

Cora nodded to acknowledge Raina's words. "I think you're here for more than that. As long as you figure out who killed Arthur, I don't care that you're lying to me." She headed back upstairs, her back stiff and ramrod straight.

The wallflower of a teenager Raina had known a few years ago had grown into a woman to be reckoned with. She shivered and headed back to her car. Would she continue to lose her friends over this passion for investigating murders?

18

A NEW GAME PLAN

Raina opened her car door and slid inside. She started the engine to head back to the downtown area. Po Po glanced up from her cell phone and then returned to her text message. Her hand reached for the seatbelt and she buckled herself in absentmindedly.

With the arrest of Mateo Riviera, the suspect list narrowed down to three people: Mia Westchester, Robert Spillman, and Bobby Spillman. However, Raina didn't think Mia would set her brother up as a scapegoat after she'd protected him by not revealing his role in the kidnapping. So she was out, but she might put pressure on the real killer because she was linked to all the suspects.

If Robert truly loved Mia, he wouldn't set up her brother either. However, Raina wasn't sure he loved Mia. Having an affair and loving someone were two different things. He might've started the affair to keep a closer eye on Arthur. Just because they were business partners for the mall development didn't mean Arthur and Robert were friends on a personal level.

And Bobby was still an enigma to Raina. Maybe she should call him up to ask for rental insurance after all, or reveal his father's affair with Mia to see how he would react.

"The Posse Club is on standby and ready for Operation Pumpkin Pie," Po Po said. "So tell us what to do, Sherlock."

Raina gave Po Po a sideways glance and returned her attention to the road. Her grandma grinned from ear to ear. With three suspects to watch over the next couple of days, Raina could use the help. However, the Posse Club had a track record of turning even the simplest task into an *I Love Lucy* episode.

"Uh, let's meet in the morning to discuss this," she finally said. "It's too late this evening to do anything." Her grandma's friends were probably in their pajamas by now. "I still have to bake goodies for the Trunk-or-Treat."

Po Po glanced at the clock on the dashboard. It was eight o'clock. "We can always get something from the Venus Cafe. And who needs sleep when you have Red Bull."

"Let's not. I need to call Officer Hopper later. We'll need the police if we want to catch the real killer."

"But the Posse—"

"Isn't enough. We can't leave the killer on the police

station's front door. Detective Sokol will claim full credit for it. I'm not helping Matthew's rival."

Po Po frowned. "I don't know. Isn't she your arch nemesis?"

Raina burst out laughing. Trust her grandmother never to take her eye off the ball. "Not anymore." She wiggled her ring finger. "Matthew's mine now. Besides, she may be open to us working together now."

"So do we call Officer Hopper and propose a plan? I'm not sure she would be on board without a lot of convincing," Po Po said.

"Well, I don't want to set myself up so she has to save the day in the middle of fighting off the killer," Raina said. She had been lucky so far in her previous investigations, but she didn't expect her luck to hold out forever.

Matthew had taught her a few basic self-defense moves and taken her to the shooting range over the summer, and he wanted her to take more lessons from an instructor. Now she regretted rejecting his idea. She didn't want to kill someone with a tweezer, but knowing how to slow someone down with one could buy her time to escape.

"I can be bait." Po Po's eyes lit up. "It's about time I get to be the star of the show."

The idea of her grandma trying to lure a killer into a confession made Raina's stomach churn with anxiety. "No."

"Why? Is it because I'm too old and too stupid?"

Raina burst out laughing. "No, it's because you have

too much energy and..." She couldn't say her grandma was a loose cannon and couldn't follow directions. "And you're too smart for your own good. You'll probably do one of your kung fu moves and end up in jail."

Po Po beamed and made a chopping motion with one hand. "Yeah, I would get thrown in jail for busting a nose or something."

"Exactly. And I don't have the bail money."

"Then it'll have to be you, Rainy."

"Maybe no one has to be bait. We'll just have to see how things shake out in the morning."

Po Po gave her a doubtful look. "Is there anything I can do to help tonight? I have this urge to do something."

Raina hesitated. She didn't want her grandma in her private business, but this concerned their town. "Could you call around to see what's keeping Matthew so busy in the Bay Area? He hasn't returned my messages, and he needs to know what Detective Sokol is doing as acting chief."

Po Po's expression turned somber. When she spoke, her voice was soft. "He's probably doing some soul searching at the moment. He was willing to set a date, but he might need to figure out how to pay for the wedding—"

"I have my inheritance—"

"He's a Chinese man. He'll have to come to terms with the money in our family."

"I'm not rich."

"While you personally might not be rich, you have access to wealth and power through the family. Our family has been wealthy merchants for generations, and here in America, we have spread to other professions."

"This is the twenty-first century. What does it matter?"

"Before marriage, it's about the two of you being in love. But afterward, the family becomes important. The in-laws are forever. He can't walk away from it, and any break is short-lived. Even with an ocean and thousands of miles between us, my in-laws have caused more than a few arguments in my marriage."

"I can't think about this right now. The killer has raised the stakes in this case. If I don't stay focused on the murder investigation, I'll miss something."

"But what about your relationship?"

Raina gripped the steering wheel. "Matthew is counting on me to keep an eye on things at the police station. There might not be a marriage to worry about if this blows up."

"It's an unfair burden on you."

"It's a sign he trusts and thinks of me as an equal. I can't let him down."

Po Po raised an eyebrow and returned to her cell phone. She mumbled something inaudible under her breath.

Raina knew her grandma was right, and Matthew probably didn't expect the length she would go to help him. But when she already had one foot through the door, she might as well jump in.

Now that she no longer had the PI internship, she might as well get used to being the next chief's secret weapon—the cupcake-baking sleuth behind the man. She made a face. This wasn't how she expected things to turn out, but a detour could be an opportunity if she squinted hard enough.

As Raina stepped into the Venus Cafe the next morning, she could sense a change in the air. The conversation was hushed, and people avoided eye contact with their neighbors. Officer Hopper waited for Raina at a table by the unlit fireplace.

Raina waved and pointed at the counter. She wanted to order her breakfast first. The line was shorter than usual, and Brenda already saw her coming. By the time she got to the counter, her pumpkin spice latte and bagel were already waiting for her.

"Can we talk later?" Raina whispered, handing over her cash.

Brenda shook her head and rang up the order. "We're closing after lunch today. Joe thinks things will get weird once it gets dark." She lowered her voice. "The serial killer press conference is making everyone nervous. I don't believe it, but I also don't want to be outside at night."

Raina grabbed her coffee and bagel and headed toward Officer Hopper. The atmosphere here at the Venus Cafe was a good gauge of the town. If they didn't find Arthur Westchester's killer soon and put an end to the serial killer rumor, people would jump at shadows.

Officer Hopper could pass for a raccoon. Her steel blue eyes were bloodshot and her blonde hair unkempt. Her uniform had more wrinkles than linen from a suitcase. She probably hadn't slept all night. The size of her coffee cup could give a normal person an ulcer.

"Rough night?" Raina asked, sliding into a chair.

Officer Hopper grunted in acknowledgment. "I just got off, but I have to be back in a few hours."

"Let's be quick then. What did you want to talk about?"

"Who is on your suspect list for Arthur Westchester's murder?"

Raina sipped her coffee to buy herself time to think. There was no point in playing coy with Officer Hopper, but neither did she want her words to go back to Detective Sokol. "What I have to say stays between us?"

Officer Hopper raised an eyebrow. "Of course."

"Last time you didn't hold up your end—"

"I won't say anything to Detective Sokol."

Raina studied Officer Hopper for a long moment, sipping her coffee again to drag it out. She told the policewoman everything she'd found out.

"We'll need help to monitor the three of them," Officer Hopper said.

Raina hesitated. She didn't want to reveal the true nature of the Posse Club to law enforcement. The senior citizen club was nothing more than a social gathering with a tendency toward mischief. "What about my grandma and her friends?"

"No! They would tip the suspects off with their antics. We must focus on two of the likely suspects."

Raina cringed inwardly. Her grandma wouldn't like being excluded from the action. "I'll put the squeeze on Mia Westchester this morning. I want to see what she might do afterward."

"Okay, I'll have a chat with Robert Spillman and see if I can shake him up," Officer Hopper said, yawning. "After I get a few hours of sleep."

"What about Bobby Spillman?" Raina asked. There was something about the man that bothered her, but she wasn't sure if she was reacting to the sleazy salesman rather than something more substantial.

"What about him? If he's in love with Mia Westchester, killing her husband gains him nothing."

"But what if he's delusional enough to think she would turn to him after her husband's death?" Raina asked.

"Then he'll go to comfort his lady love soon enough. And if he doesn't confess his love, then he had no motive to kill Arthur."

Raina nodded slowly. It made sense for Bobby to console Mia. It would be too good of an opportunity to miss. So by watching Mia, Raina would essentially be keeping an eye on Bobby as well.

"So is Mateo Riviera charged with Arthur Westchester's murder?" Raina asked. "The anonymous caller and planted cell phone seems like it came from the plot of a B-rated movie."

Officer Hopper covered her face with her hands. "I don't even want to talk about this circus act. Detective Sokol broke almost every policy and violated so many laws."

"Well, maybe you can get promoted to detective after this. You have enough experience helping Matthew the last few years." Raina wasn't sure if this was true, but anyone had to be better than Detective Sokol.

Officer Hopper glanced up from her hands, brows wrinkled in thought. "I've never given it much thought. When you work for a small department, there isn't much room for upward mobility."

"How long have you been in your current position?"

"Almost six years. With budget cuts, the higher positions kept getting cut. Sooner or later, we'll end up relying on the county sheriff for the investigative work. We'll be lucky if we have enough staff for traffic control."

Raina frowned. This seemed more like mismanagement of city funds than anything else. Was this why the city agreed to the mall development at the edge of town when there were sufficient mom-and-pop stores in town?

Officer Hopper stood, distracting Raina from her thoughts. "Sounds like we have a game plan. Call me if anything changes."

19

THE POSSE CLUB

After Officer Hopper left, Raina finished her breakfast and left for the senior center to attend the Posse Club meeting. She wanted to get on with the investigation, but if she didn't show, her grandma would feel slighted in front of her friends.

Officer Hopper was right. Involving the senior citizens would be dangerous. The Posse Club were a motley crew that needed babysitting more than anything else—and this included her grandma. She needed to give them assignments that made them feel important with a small taste of excitement and no chance of danger. That was a tall order.

At least she didn't have to worry about her niece. Lila was with another one of her grandma's friends. Raina should feel a small tinge of guilt, but the child was being spoiled by cookies and *Barney*. And she was taking Lila to the Trunk-or-Treat later this evening.

A few minutes later, she surveyed the crew in front of her in the small conference room at the senior center. The room held a round table big enough to seat eight. The chairs were mismatched like they came from the discarded remains of dining sets the senior citizen couldn't get rid of when they moved in. The big picture window's curtains were shut to keep out prying eyes from their top secret club meeting.

The five club members talked among themselves and munched on cookies. Frank Small's dark brown face gave nothing away, though his eyes gleamed with excitement. He was Po Po's wingman, and Raina often counted on him to keep her grandma grounded. He was ex-military, so he understood following directions and not engaging the suspect.

Maggie Louie was her fiancé's grandma and half blind. And yet, she arrived with a platter of cookies and sweet bread for the club meeting. Every time she shifted, Raina could smell vanilla and lemon drops. Maybe Maggie could bribe the desk clerk at the police station with food?

The elderly gentleman was the same one in the life vest during the *Gangnam Style* dance. Raina forgot his name as soon as he said it. The woman was his Korean wife. They were one of those rare couples in the senior community still together and enjoyed good health after fifty years. They held hands under the table.

Her grandma was in fine form. She had switched from Korean hipster to army mode—pink combat fatigues and a giant paintball gun strapped to her back with two more plastic water guns on either side of her hip. Knowing her grandma, Raina suspected the toy guns weren't filled with water. While they probably weren't filled with acid, she wouldn't be surprised if the liquid stunk, stung, or burned.

Po Po rapped at the table, and the conversation died down. "Thank you for volunteering to be part of Operation Pumpkin Pie. We'll use the buddy system for this. Frank, you're with Maggie. The Lovebirds are on one team, and I'm with Rainy. Do we have our walkie-talkies ready?"

The club members patted bags or pockets to show all were in working order. Po Po pulled out a small black box and slid it across the table to Raina. "Your show now, hon?"

Raina cleared her throat. "Frank and Maggie, you're to keep an eye on Detective Sokol. We need to know what he's up to next. Talk to Donna if you need to."

Frank and Maggie nodded.

"Lovebirds," Raina said, using the same nickname as her grandma. "I want you to keep an eye on Mateo Riviera. He should be released from police custody soon. They can't hold him over twenty-four hours without charging him. I want to know what he does next and who he talks to."

The couple nodded, smiling at each other.

"Po Po and I will put the squeeze on Mia Westchester. Officer Hopper will be doing the same to Robert Spillman," Raina said.

"Who's watching Bobby Spillman?" Po Po asked.

Raina shrugged. "There's not enough people, and I don't want anyone alone. We'll have to wait and see what happens next. If Bobby killed Arthur Westchester to get rid of a romantic rival, then he would try to get more face time with Mia."

"What if his interest in Mia is only a smokescreen?" Mrs. Lovebird asked.

Raina hadn't considered this angle before. "Let's see how the others do first." Maybe she should see how Bobby reacted to news of his father's affair with Mia. It would be interesting to have the three of them in a room together.

"Let's try to get back by five, so we can get ready for the performance tonight," Po Po said.

"We'll have a small crowd tonight with a serial killer loose," Maggie said, picking up her white cane.

"Big or small, we're still gonna get our groove on," Po Po said, gyrating her hips.

Raina covered a smile with her hand. She hoped someone didn't end up in the hospital for breaking a hip. How would she explain it the doctors?

The Posse Club members saluted and left. Raina was surprised no one argued about the assignment. Maybe most of them wanted something to pass the time. Regardless, she was happy the teams wouldn't be in real danger...unless the killer began to feel the squeeze.

On their way back to the lobby, Po Po's cell phone

rang. She glanced at it and handed it to Raina. "It's for you. I need to use the restroom."

Raina glanced at the display on the phone. The caller was Toni Moody. "Hello. This is Raina Sun."

"What's wrong with your phone? I've been calling you all morning," Toni said.

"Long story. I don't have a cell phone until I stop by a cell phone store in Sacramento."

"Sacramento?"

"The local one wouldn't sell me insurance on my phone anymore."

"Why—" Toni cut herself off. "Sorry. I don't need to know. Can you stop by the office this afternoon?"

Raina could make the time, but time was of the essence with the killer pulling puppet strings in the background. And after their last conversation, she wasn't eager to have another one with her former boss. "What is this about? Did I forget a paycheck?"

Toni paused for half a heartbeat. If Raina wasn't listening for it, she would have missed it. Her former boss wanted something from her.

"Mia Westchester stopped by the office this morning," Toni said. "She wants to hire us to find out who framed her brother."

Raina should have felt a sense of validation, but instead, it was too late. Somehow along the way, she'd crossed a threshold. She didn't like being at the forefront of an investigation. If she got her PI license, the bad guys would know she was coming after them, and this could jeopardize her safety. And besides, Toni had abandoned Raina when she most needed her.

"I'm busy for the next couple days," Raina said.

"I see," Toni said. She paused for a moment. "Are you sure? I had such high hopes for you."

"I did too. I need to take care of my grandma and her friends, so I can't make the time."

"Looks like I'll have to do this on my own then. Good luck, Raina."

Toni hesitated. "Same to you."

Raina hung up, staring at the display on her grandma's phone until it turned black. Would it be melodramatic to say she could feel the rush of air from the door slamming shut in front of her? Why didn't she try to keep this door open a little longer? What if she regretted this decision later?

Footsteps approached her. "Everything okay?" Po Po asked.

Raina glanced up to see her grandma studying her with concern. She told Po Po what was said in the conversation with Toni. "I don't know if it's my pride taking over, or if I made an informed decision."

Po Po shrugged. "You're overthinking this. Since no one will come to any physical harm from your decision, I say we move on. Besides, now we have an excuse to talk to Mia Westchester. She still thinks you work for Toni Moody."

"You're devious." One corner of Raina's lips curled. Her grandma usually had things right. "I like it. Let's roll."

Raina parked in front of the Westchester McMansion driveway. The lawn held lumpy piles of fallen leaves and half-filled black bags as if the gardener left in the middle of his job. The curtains were drawn without a single peek at the outside world. A large black wreath adorned the front door.

Po Po dug in her purse and pulled out a Kevlar vest. "For the gun."

"Are you wearing one?" Raina asked.

Po Po lifted up her sweater, exposing her vest. "All set."

Raina peeled off her sweater and put on the vest without an argument. Sometimes it was much easier to humor her grandma. At close range, the Kevlar vest was probably more for show than anything else against a shotgun. When she put her sweater back on, she looked as if she gained ten pounds. Yep, Mia Westchester wouldn't notice the vest at all. Raina suppressed a sigh.

Po Po pulled out two plastic bags filled with doggie treats from her purse. She shook them with a wide grin on her face. "One is laced with marijuana and the other with Prozac. One of these is bound to mellow the dog."

Raina's eyes widened. Oh, no. They were going to get shot. "What if you end up poisoning the dog?"

"I consulted with a vet and got his okay on this. Mia will probably thank us for solving her dog problem." Po Po beamed like she solved their problem.

Raina didn't even know how to respond so she

didn't. The problem wasn't the dog. It was the owner who would sic the dog on them or put a hole in their bodies. Unlike the rest of the family who thought Po Po might be losing it, Raina believed her grandma was perfectly aware of what she was doing and using her age as a cover up when needed.

20

PICK YOUR POISON

They strolled down the driveway and rang the doorbell. A few minutes later, Mia cracked open the door. Her face was puffy, and her eyes were red. Either she had been crying, or she had a bad cold.

"What happened to you?" Po Po asked.

"Po Po!" Raina addressed Mia. "Please excuse my grandma. Sometimes she's a little old and senile." She shot her grandmother a sharp look.

Mia blew her nose and waved them in. "I can't believe Toni Moody sent the two you instead of coming here to meet with me herself."

Raina and Po Po followed Mia into the mansion. The side table was upright, but the shredded curtains were still in place. As they crossed the foyer, Po Po shook her bag of doggie treats.

Mia leaned close to Raina and lowered her voice. "What is she doing?"

"She thinks your dog has anxiety," Raina whispered back.

"My vet told me the same thing. He's taking Prozac and seeing a pet psychiatrist once a week."

Raina's brows rose to her hairline. *You got to be kidding me.*

"Hey, don't judge. My dog is my baby."

Raina didn't know how to respond. Growing up in the Bay Area in tight quarters meant there was no room for a pet. And later when she moved into her grandmother's house, she was reeling from her father's death. She'd never developed an affinity for animals. "We all have our weaknesses," she finally said.

Mia appeared mollified by her response and led them into a small sitting room. She sank into the love seat and curled her legs underneath her. Next to her on the cushion was a pile of crumpled Kleenex. Raina and Po Po sat on the stiff sofa across from Mia.

Raina pulled out a small notebook from her purse. "Toni said you wanted us to find out who framed your brother. This person could be your husband's killer. Do you have any suspect in mind?"

Mia crossed her arms. "If I knew who killed my husband and framed my brother, why would I need to hire you?"

Raina ignored Mia's tone. "Your brother is in possession of the cell phone that was used to call your husband the night before his death. Do you know anything about this call?"

"He took the call in his office. I don't have the passcode to his cell phone, so I couldn't check to see who called him," Mia said. "He was out of sorts all night like he just got bad news. Probably something that will stop the construction on one of the projects." She shrugged. "Something is always threatening to shut down construction."

"Can't you call the cell phone company to get the information?"

"I'm not on the phone plan, so I have no access to his account."

Raina paused in her note taking. By not being in a family plan together, it made hiding things from each other much easier. "What was the business relationship like between your husband and Robert Spillman? How long were they partners together?"

"Robert is a filthy snake. He's a fu—" Mia cut off her tirade. She closed her eyes and pressed her hands to her temples.

While Mia took several deep breaths, Raina raised an eyebrow at her grandma. Po Po glanced at the pile of tissues and mouthed "break-up" in Chinese.

Raina nodded in agreement. But why would Robert break things off with Mia on the eve of her brother getting framed for the murder? Mia must have called Robert shortly after she found out herself.

If Raina were in Robert's shoes, she would have kept up with the affair to keep Mia from flapping her mouth...unless he felt that he got away with murder.

"How did the partnership form between Arthur and Robert?" Raina asked.

Mia opened her eyes, glancing at the ceiling. "Both Arthur and Robert wanted to buy the family land, and I had to sell it to pay the taxes. So they formed a partnership to reduce the risk from the purchase, but they were always at odds on what to do with the land."

"What do you mean at odds?" Po Po asked.

"Arthur wanted to develop it, but Robert wanted to preserve it as open space."

"Do you know that Bobby still carries a torch for you?" Po Po asked.

Mia rolled her eyes. "The guy is delusional. We only dated for a few months before his arrest."

"Bobby seems to be under the impression that Robert didn't help him during his arrest," Raina said.

"Robert hired the best lawyer in town, but Bobby was caught red-handed. He blames his father for letting him get thrown in jail. And Robert still carries a lot of that guilt with him." Mia paused thoughtfully. "Sometimes I wonder if I made the wrong choice."

"Wrong choice in selling the land or the husband?" Raina asked.

"Maybe both," Mia whispered.

"Did you love your husband?" Po Po asked.

"I did until he went ahead with plans to develop the mall," Mia said. "Both Robert and I were against it. We didn't think he would go through the permitting process so quickly with City Hall. He must have greased palms to push it through."

"How come Robert didn't offer to buy Arthur out?" Raina asked.

"Unlike Arthur who was born into his wealth, Robert made his from owning several dry cleaners. When the recession hit, it hit him pretty hard," Mia said.

"Did Arthur offer to buy Robert out?" Raina asked.

Mia rolled her eyes and huffed. "During the recession? Why would Arthur sink more money into this? In business, you don't throw more money into a deal that might not pan out," she said slowly as if she were talking to a child.

Raina wasn't offended. People who underestimated her tended to ramble on, revealing a secret or two.

"Of course, no one expected the recession to last this long. I thought he might offer to give my family land back to me." Mia's smile was brittle, but it didn't reach her eyes. "I shouldn't have signed the prenuptial agreement."

"Did he leave you anything?" Raina asked.

"He left me this house, and the mortgage that went with it," Mia said.

"So who's getting his money?" Po Po asked.

"This lawyer called to say it was going to a distant cousin in Georgia," Mia said. "I spent the last few years with Arthur, and I get nothing."

"Isn't there equity in this house?" Raina asked.

Mia laughed, a bitter and harsh sound. "I owe more on it than it's worth. I couldn't even pay the gardener to finish the lawn. Arthur really screwed me."

Raina glanced at her grandma. Now was the time

to push Mia to see how she would crack. "Maybe he knew you were screwing around with Robert."

Mia stiffened. She turned her head slowly like a doll to stare at Raina. "I hired you to find out who framed my brother. I didn't hire you to gossip about my personal life."

From the corner of her eye, Raina could see the wide smile on her grandma's face. She wiggled her eyebrows to goad Raina on.

"Your personal life is related to everything. You're the link to all the men in this case," Raina said.

"It's like you're the black widow in the middle of a web," Po Po said.

Mia shot her grandma a dirty look. "I didn't kill my husband, and I'm no black widow." She stood. "It's time for you to go."

Raina followed Mia to the foyer, trotting beside her. "What do you know about the mass grave on your family land?"

Mia stopped in her tracks, and Po Po ran into her back. Her grandma apologized and sidestepped. Mia glared at her grandma and resumed her march. "I don't know what you're talking about."

"You haven't heard about the press conference from the police? They found a mass burial at your property. They think a serial murderer is on the loose," Po Po said, keeping up with the younger woman.

Mia held the front door open for them. "I can't believe I subjected myself to this. You're done. I want

Moody Investigation off this case, and you can keep the retainer." Her tone was brisk and flat.

Raina stood at the threshold, considering her words. Toni would be livid when she found out Raina had cost her a client. There would be no going back for Raina with her tail between her legs to beg for the internship. "I never said I worked for Toni. You made the assumption that I did."

Mia blinked, her face turning blotchy with anger. "Poe!" She whistled. "Come here, boy!"

The floor shook from the mad gallop of a black Lab the size of a miniature horse. The dog came into view in the hallway. His mouth was open, and his tongue flopped from the corner of his mouth, globs of saliva dribbling to the floor with each step.

Raina's mouth went dry with fear. The dog probably wouldn't bite her, but she didn't want to find out either. She willed her feet to move, but they were glued to the floor.

Po Po tossed the bags of doggie treats at the black Lab, but he didn't spare them a glance. He raced toward them like he wanted a new chew toy.

"Oh, sh—" A sharp pain in Raina's arm cut her off.

Po Po clutched Raina's forearm, her nails digging into the skin, and dragged Raina outside.

Mia slammed the door shut after them. It rattled as if a massive body rammed into it. The dog barked and slammed into the door again.

They ran for the car. When they got inside, Raina hit the locks. Their breaths came out in noisy puffs.

Raina's heart raced, and she leaned against the steering wheel.

"What do we do now?" Po Po asked.

Raina glanced over at the passenger seat. Her grandma looked composed and relaxed. "I'm about to die from a heart attack, and you're not even breaking a sweat."

"I get plenty of practice running from dogs and the police," Po Po said, reaching into her purse and pulling out her cell phone.

Raina started the engine. "Now we wait at a less conspicuous spot. She's bound to go to Robert for help. She'll play the damsel in distress to win him back, though I don't think it will work."

21

A HAUNTING GOOD TIME

As someone tapped her shoulder, Raina jerked awake. She blinked and glanced over the dashboard of her car to peer at the Westchester McMansion. The same lights were still on, and no other movement in the neighborhood.

"We have to leave to make it back for the Trunk-or-Treat," Po Po said from the passenger seat, lowering her bird watching binoculars from her eyes. "I can't believe we spent the last three hours here."

"You're the one who wants to play detective. Surveillance is part of the job," Raina said, stretching her arms to loosen up the knots in her upper back. She started the engine.

"Let me check in with the others," Po Po said, pulling out her walkie-talkie. She pressed a button, and it crackled to life. "Red Ninja reporting in. The Black Widow is in the nest. How are things at your end, Big and Tiny?"

"The Court Jester is home playing with his babies," Frank said. "We're already at base camp setting up our booth. We've also got the Little Monkey with us."

"White Doves, are you there?" Po Po asked.

"All is clear," said Mrs. Lovebird. "We're on our way back to base camp too."

Po Po turned off the walkie-talkie in disgust. "We wasted our entire day. We didn't even learn anything new."

Raina signaled her intent to make a left turn. "We learned plenty. We found out Mia didn't know about the mass burial, but Robert did. We might have our motive for Arthur's death."

Po Po popped a can of Red Bull. An empty can rolled against her feet when Raina made the turn. "You don't think his preservation stance is real?"

"Do you see any other indication of environmental activism from Robert? But I believe Mateo is an activist. He has a reputation for it, and it's only normal for him to want to retain the open space on his family land."

"We lost our ancestral home and farmlands when my father died. The wives sold everything and divided the money among themselves. If my father hadn't set aside a store for me, I would have ended up homeless at sixteen."

Raina glanced at Po Po and returned her attention to the road. "I'm surprised the Little Emperor and his mom didn't end up with everything."

"My brother died in his infancy. I was the closest

my father had to a son because I was the boldest girl," Po Po said with a hint of satisfaction in her voice.

Raina wasn't surprised her grandma ended up on her feet in the end. "I can't have you getting into a snit because I'm not spending enough time with you."

"What are you talking about?"

"You've seemed irritated since my engagement to Matthew."

"I'm upset because you're letting him dictate the terms of your relationship again."

Raina blinked. She had it all wrong again. Not surprising.

"Don't worry about me," Po Po continued. "I'm not sitting in my condo, picking my nose until you show up. I have plenty to keep me busy."

Raina parked in the half-full parking lot, and they got out.

"You have a costume, Rainy?" Po Po asked.

"Uh...am I supposed to have one?"

"Don't worry, I got you covered," Po Po said.

As Raina handed a miniature chocolate bar to the little witch in front of her from inside the Posse Club's booth, her eyes tracked the movement of Bobby Spillman across the recreation room of the senior center. He mingled with the crowd, handing out his business card and treats from a black bag slung over one shoulder, probably drumming up leads for his insurance company. The only concession he gave to the occasion was a light-up ghost on the lapel of his black suit.

Raina shifted, and a cold draft slid from her back-side up her spine. Her grandma had her covered, all right, in the costume department. Or maybe the better word was *exposed*.

Her white seventies geometric disco dress was several inches shorter than the rest of the ladies in the dance group, and the stilettos on the go-go boots were a couple of inches too high. At least she kept her cotton briefs instead of the black butt floss her grandma wanted her to wear. There were moments when she wondered if her grandma had been a pimp in her previous life.

Raina elbowed her grandma and gestured in Bobby's direction. "Look who's here."

Robert Spillman dressed as Mark Antony approached his son. Bobby scowled at his father and stalked off in the opposite direction before they had a chance to speak. Relations between father and son had apparently deteriorated in the last few days. Raina was tempted to go after Bobby to lend a friendly ear to his complaints. After all, she had parental issues of her own and could relate.

Po Po elbowed her back and gestured in the oppo-site direction. "Look at the eye candy heading this way."

Raina turned her head, and her heart skipped a beat. Matthew strolled toward them in a brown wig, black tuxedo, cape, cane, and fangs. His brown eyes sparkled, highlighting the golden flecks in them. She glanced down to hide her broad smile. It wouldn't do to seem too eager, though she wanted to vault over the booth and run straight into his arms.

"I think he'll like your dress," Po Po said, winking. She straightened her own teal-colored tuxedo jacket. She shoved her mini pumpkin launcher at Raina. "Hold on to this for me. I don't want it lying around the booth. Be careful. There's a pumpkin in the barrel."

Raina glanced at the launcher and small purse. "My bag might not look the same after getting stretched out for your toy."

Po Po shrugged. "I'll get you a new one the next time we go shopping. Take it. I need to make my way to the stage. We're next."

Raina couldn't say no. If the social committee found out her grandma traveled with a weapon of mass destruction, she could be banned from outings for the rest of the year. And if Matthew found out about the launcher, he would have to confiscate it for public safety. Either outcome would upset her grandma. She shoved the launcher and the two mini pumpkins into her purse. It bulged like she was hiding a massive vibrator, and it weighed a ton.

When she glanced up again, Matthew stood across from her. He held out his hand. "Come, my lovely. Let's dance."

She rolled her eyes and laughed at his fake accent. "I haven't seen you all week, and you haven't returned any of my calls. And I'm supposed to swoon over your fake Transylvanian accent?"

He pretended to brush a piece of lint off his shoulder. "You're meant to swoon over my outfit. I better put on my mask." He pulled a black mask from his pocket and slipped it on. It covered half his face.

Raina grabbed her purse and stepped around the booth but didn't grab onto his arm. If he needed to disguise himself, this meant he didn't want people to identify him. He was probably on the job. If she clung onto him, she would come off as a hussy or make it easy for the community to guess his identity.

He glanced at her lumpy purse and raised an eyebrow.

"This is what happens when you leave me alone. I have to take care of business myself," Raina said.

They strolled through the crowd of forty or fifty families, each towing two or three kids. Even during holidays like Thanksgiving or Christmas, the center wouldn't see a turnout like this when adult children came to take Mom or Dad out to lunch. Maybe the serial murderer rumor had people seeking an indoor activity for their families on Halloween.

The senior citizens had gone all out, decorating the entire center and the large recreation room into a haunted house. The long plastic tables were folded and set aside along the walls. In the middle of the recreation room were two long rows of booths sponsored by the various senior citizen clubs, community organizations, and a few businesses. At the far end of the room was a raised platform for the talent show.

Matthew and Raina headed away from the platform so they could speak without shouting at each other. He apologized for not returning her calls because he left his phone charger behind. If this wasn't a sign they were meant for each other, Raina didn't know what it was. She filled him in on the investigation, and he listened without comment until she was done.

"All three suspects will be here tonight," Matthew said.

Raina's eyes widened, and she glanced around. She'd seen Bobby and Robert Spillman. Now that she was looking, a Paris mime followed them at a discreet distance. She squinted at the Cleopatra standing next to a large prize wheel three booths away from them. Was that Mia Westchester? She glanced at the banner over the booth: Westchester Development. Yep, Cleopatra was Mia. Did she coordinate costumes with Robert before their break-up? Or maybe they made up in the last few hours?

"Stop that. You're going to alert them to the police presence in the room," Matthew said.

"Are you in a sting operation?" Raina whispered. She wondered how Mia, Robert, and Bobby would react to being in the same room.

Matthew shook his head. "We're here to keep an eye on things. We have no reason to believe any of the suspects would do anything."

For some reason, Raina couldn't help but feel disappointed in his response. She knew her fiancé was a methodical man when it came to his investigations, checking all the boxes and making sure to follow up with all the leads. After she told him about all the legwork she had done, she thought he would be ready for action.

Matthew squeezed her shoulder briefly and dropped his arm. "Joanna Hopper told Bobby about Robert and Mia having an affair. Maybe you should tell Mia that Robert is looking for her. I'll go get us a lemonade."

Raina returned his smile and straightened her short dress. She could read between the lines. There was no sting operation, but the police wanted to kick the hornet's nest to see what would happen. And since the cops couldn't officially do the kicking, it was up to her. Cool beans. She didn't mind being the instrument of justice. She strutted the short distance to Mia with her battle-ready smile on.

22

A MOONLIT STROLL

"Mia, your Mark Antony is looking for you. He asked if I saw you a few minutes ago," Raina said.

A child dressed as Dorothy from *The Wizard of Oz* scowled at Raina. "Hey, no cutting, lady."

Raina held up both hands, palms open. "Sorry. I'm not here to spin the prize wheel."

Mia chewed her lower lip. "I'm not in the mood to talk to him now."

"Hey, where's my prize?" Dorothy said, glancing from Mia to Raina.

Mia dropped a lollipop into her bag. "Off you go now."

"A lollipop? What kind of cheap prize is this?" Dorothy dropped the candy back into Mia's treat bucket and stomped off.

"I hope she gets a stomachache from the candy,"

Mia mumbled. She turned and spoke to the man behind her.

Raina shifted from foot to foot and glanced around her. Matthew watched her from the line for the lemonade booth. She winked at him, but he either didn't see her, or he pretended they didn't know each other. Real smooth. She had to be more like him when she was on assignment.

"Why is Robert looking for me?" Mia asked.

Raina spun around to find Mia standing next to her. Her pulse kicked up a notch. Time to put the squeeze on the players in this game. "Bobby Spillman found out about your affair with his father."

Mia's face turned ashen, and she clutched her hands to her chest. "What did you do? Why did you tell him?" she whispered.

Raina blinked at Mia's fear. It seemed rather excessive. "Did he kill your husband? Is that why you're afraid of him?"

"No, you meddling fool! I don't know if he killed my husband, but his father might be in danger."

"You think he'll kill Robert Spillman?" Raina asked. What did she miss?

"Nooo," Mia dragged the word out, staring at Raina as if she were a crazed bag lady. "They'll probably have a huge argument, and Robert will end up in the hospital."

"I don't understand what you're saying," Raina asked, feeling incredibly dense. If Bobby weren't the killer, why did Mia react like Raina put Robert's life in danger?

"Because Robert has high blood pressure, and the stress from the argument will send him to the hospital. He'd be lucky if he didn't have a heart attack. Thanks a lot."

Raina winced as if Mia had slapped her. Her face grew hot. Robert couldn't be the killer if he had health issues. He wouldn't be able to bash Arthur in with a rake without dropping from the stress of a murder. "I'm so—"

Mia stomped off into the crowd, ignoring Raina's apology. The Paris mime followed Mia. The speakers blared "Hey, sexy lady."

Raina should see her grandma's performance. The crowd seemed to have grown, and the thought of fighting it to get to the front of the room was daunting. Her back and feet ached from the stiletto boots. She wanted nothing more than to go home.

She hobbled toward the entrance of the recreation room, hoping the fresh air would cool her down. Leaning against the wall, she took off her boots and wiggled her toes. Why did she subject herself to this misery to make her grandma happy? Blisters and ingrown toenails from high heels weren't attractive no matter what anyone said.

A hand holding an iced strawberry lemonade appeared in her peripheral vision. Raina glanced over and smiled. Matthew shook the cup until the ice rattled inside the plastic.

She slurped a quarter of the drink in one breath. The icy liquid was the perfect combination of tang and sweetness. She pressed the cold cup on her forehead, enjoying the condensation even though it probably looked ridiculous.

"Outside?" Matthew asked, still in his fake accent. She didn't know he enjoyed role-playing like her grandma did.

Raina nodded. As she followed him, she took smaller sips of the lemonade. It would be rude to finish the cup before he got a chance to have any.

They strolled to the small community garden at the side of the building. Wood trellises covered in grapevines surrounded the small area and created a private space at the busy senior center. They sat down at one of the stone benches. The landscaping light was dim and intimate. Crickets chirped around them.

Raina could think of a number of things she would rather do with her fiancé at the moment than discuss the murder investigation. But he wouldn't want her to withhold information that might help him.

"Matthew, I know who killed Arthur Westchester," Raina whispered. "It has to be Bobby Spillman." She told him about Mia's reaction when she mentioned Bobby finding out about her affair with his father. "With Robert's health issues, I doubt he had the strength to kill Arthur so violently at the pumpkin patch."

"Why?" Matthew asked. It came out sounding like *Vhy*.

Raina chewed her lower lip. This was the part that was pure speculation. "It probably has to do with the burial insurance he's selling to the senior citizens."

Matthew gave her a doubtful look.

"I'm sure the elderly with family around got the white glove service as advertised. But for those without family, it's not hard to dig a hole and dump them in," Raina said, her mouth twisting with distaste. "It cost more than five thousand dollars to get cremated these days. How does his insurance stay in business if it can scatter your ashes in Hawaii for this amount?"

Matthew rolled his hand to encourage her to continue.

"His father must know about his activities. Why else would he partner with Arthur Westchester and actively discourage the development of the old pumpkin patch?"

His eyes widened, and he sat back onto his bench as if he were in shock. His hand flew to his chest, and Raina noticed the ghost lapel pin for the first time. It wasn't lit up, which might be why she didn't notice it before. Matthew wasn't wearing a pin.

All the air rushed out of Raina's head until she grew dizzy with fear. The hair on the back of her neck and arms rose, and she tried to suppress a shiver. Sitting next to her was Bobby Spillman. She was alone in the dark with Arthur Westchester's killer, and she'd told him everything.

How could she have mistaken the two men for each other? Matthew would never have lead her to an isolated garden when there was a killer on the loose. He would tell her there was safety in numbers.

Her pride had put her in a dangerous situation because she couldn't wait to tell Matthew how clever she was for figuring out the killer's identity. She was an idiot.

Raina stood, clutching her boots and purse in front of her. "Let me go get you something." The words tumbled out in one breath.

She backed away from him, praying she wouldn't trip on something. She saw the tuxedo and the mask and assumed this man was Matthew. Bobby didn't even smell like her fiancé. She was such a fool to let him maneuver her into this remote area.

If she were to turn around and run, Bobby would be on her like a wolf on prey. With the tight dress, she couldn't outrun him. They had been gone long enough that Matthew was probably looking for her. She had to stall until the police showed up.

Bobby stood, towering over her. He spat out the fake fangs. The world became still like even the crickets were afraid to disturb what would happen next.

Please don't remove the mask, Raina prayed. Once she knew his true identity, there would be no going back to pretending he was Matthew.

Bobby reached for the mask, and Raina grabbed his hand to stop him.

"Honey, I don't understand why Bobby doesn't make a run for it." Raina said conversationally, surprised her voice didn't wobble with strain. "If he left town or even the state, he could get away with murder. There's no real evidence to charge him with anything."

Bobby went still and lowered his hand. He glanced over Raina's shoulders as if considering her words. She kept her eyes on his face and unzipped her purse. Her shaking hand curled around the mini pumpkin launcher. She had only one shot, so she needed to make it count.

"If I leave, the old man wins. If he had saved me the first time, I wouldn't be in my current situation." Bobby ripped off his mask. "Let's see if Papa will save me this time." He grabbed Raina's hair, pulling her close to him.

She jerked the pumpkin launcher at his face and pulled the trigger.

Nothing happened.

"What is that thing?" Bobby said, laughing at the metal tube.

He swatted it away from his face, almost knocking it out of Raina's hand.

"Let go of me!" Raina yelled, wincing at the pain. She tightened her grip on the pumpkin launcher, pointed it at Bobby, and pulled the trigger again.

Wha-amp!

Crunch!

Bobby screamed and released her hair. His hands formed a protective shield around his nose and blood gushed around his hands and ran down his arms. Raina took a step back and swung the stiletto boots at his groin. He stumbled and fell to the ground, clutching at his groin. His screams became a shriek.

Raina turned and fled. She hitched up her dress until it became a tube around her upper thighs to lengthen her strides. The lights from the senior center glittered against the darkness. Her breaths sounded loud in her ears, and her lungs burned. Running for her life was nothing like a leisurely morning jog.

A shadow moved away from the wall, and Bobby stood between her and safety. His mask was back in place, probably to hide the bloody nose. Raina screamed in frustration and tightened her grip on her purse. She wasn't slowing down. Either she went through him or bounced off him. Behind her, the dark parking lot promised even more danger.

Raina waited until they were a couple of feet from each other and swung her purse, aiming for his face again. His eyes widened in surprise, and he stumbled back. There was no blood on his face.

"Rainy," Matthew called out, his arm raised to block her.

She released her hold on the strap, and the purse whacked his shoulder. Before he could recover, Raina threw her arms around his neck. "It was Bobby," she said, her voice hitching. "He's in the garden."

23

WEDDING BELLS

Cassie and Benson showed up to pick up Lila from Po Po's condo the next morning. The couple seemed more rested. While Benson loaded up the gear in the car, Raina had a few undisturbed minutes with her sister in the kitchen.

The long weekend had extended to almost a full week. Raina had hoped the time away from the daily routine had helped the couple recall why they got married in the first place.

"The time away was productive?" Raina asked, pouring her sister a cup of green tea.

Cassie tapped on the countertop three times to thank Raina like they did in the old country. "We're not getting a divorce. Benson threatened to stop going to marriage counseling unless I find a part-time activity outside the home. He wants me to leave home every day. He said the nanny could take care of Lila."

Raina's eyes widened. Whoa, her brother-in-law

was one smart cookie. By demanding Cassie fill her time, Benson must think the solution lay in staying busy. "Uh, what exactly is the problem in your marriage?"

"I don't even know where to begin. I feel like I'm always being left behind."

Raina didn't understand what her sister meant, and probably didn't have time to get the full explanation. "What are you planning to do then?"

Cassie squared her shoulders. "I'll do what it takes to save my marriage. I'm joining Mom's Ladies Justice League."

Raina sipped her tea to hide her smile. "That's the club Mom joined after Hudson's arrest, right?"

"Yes. There's a cloud of secrecy around it. No website. No brochure." Cassie smirked. "I guess this shouldn't be surprising. After all, Po Po is one of the founding members."

Now, this got Raina's attention. "Really? She never talks about it."

"You're not supposed to." Cassie lowered her voice. "That's why it's a secret and by invite only."

Raina blinked in confusion. How come she hadn't been invited to this club? Were the other women in her family members too? "Who invited you?"

"Mom."

Of course, their mother would invite Cassie. She had always been the favorite.

"Hon, are you ready to go?" Benson called out from the living room.

Cassie set down her teacup and hugged Raina. "Thanks for everything, Mei Mei."

Raina returned the hug, blinking at the burning behind her eyes. Her older sister rarely used Raina's formal title in the family. Mei Mei meant little sister in Chinese. "It's nothing. We enjoyed having the Little Tornado with us. She—at least—follows the rules. Unlike our grandma."

They chuckled and went to join everyone in the living room. After Cassie and her family left, Raina asked her grandma about the Ladies Justice League. But Po Po's garbled explanation that the club was a charity to help abused women only made Raina more curious. After all, if this club were an average charity, there wouldn't be any need for secrecy.

A FEW DAYS LATER, Raina was on a ladder removing the black and orange streamers from the recreation room. The cleanup would take another day at this rate. The senior citizens didn't move at the speed of light, and many of them had to take naps in between. It had taken them a month to set the place up for the Trunk-or-Treat.

Or maybe they were playing her for a fool because she often got volunteered to do the grunt work. Her grandma and her cronies were on the raised platform. They were supposed to do the tear down, but instead, it looked like they were standing around chatting.

"Hey, government employees, get back to work," Raina called out.

They grinned up at her and waved.

Raina rolled her eyes. Yep, she was the fool, all right.

Matthew strolled in and headed straight for her.

Po Po and her friends glanced at the clock on the wall and called out "break time" and left the room.

Raina climbed down the ladder and waited for her fiancé. Matthew moved with the easy grace of someone who knew his worth. Bobby Spillman darted around like a furtive rat looking for his next meal. How could she have mistaken the two men for each other?

In hindsight, she blamed the discovery of the killer's identity for clouding her judgment. She had wanted to prove to Matthew she was as clever as him and forgot about her safety. This was a lesson she hoped never to forget.

Matthew glanced around the empty room. "Are they working you like a dog?"

"Yep."

"Are you getting anything out of this?"

"Nope."

"Wow, you're easy."

"So I've been told."

He rubbed his chin to hide his smile. "I got the same bargain as you."

"Cleaning up after Detective Sokol?"

"Yep."

"Are you getting a promotion out of it?"

"Nope."

Raina kissed his cheek. "Man, you're easy."

Matthew wrapped an arm around her waist and pretended to leer at her. "Since we're both so easy, how come we still have clothes on?"

She laughed and pushed him away. "And give the old folks here a heart-attack? No, thanks." She lowered her voice. "Maybe later."

He winked. "It's a date."

"Did Bobby confess to the murder?" Raina asked, reaching for a nearby trash bag.

Matthew took the trash bag from her and held it open. "Surprisingly, he did."

Raina began gathering the streamers on the floor. "Why was it surprising? He did the deed."

"We don't have any solid evidence against him, and it will take the county lab a few days to finish their work. He could say you attacked him—"

"He grabbed me first."

Matthew's eyes hardened. "He's in a holding cell now."

Raina dumped the streamers into the trash bag. "Stand down, tough guy. I'm okay now. Has Robert Spillman come to see him?"

"Yes, with a lawyer in tow."

"I think Robert invested in the mall development to stop the construction because he suspected something was wrong with his son's business. He might have started the affair with Mia to keep an eye on things."

"You're probably right."

"I don't understand why he didn't ask his son about it instead of going around this big bush."

"Because they're men. Can you imagine the two of them sitting down and having a heart-to-heart chat?"

Raina snorted. "Robert should have brought a therapist along too. Bobby has some serious daddy issues."

Matthew raised an eyebrow.

Raina ignored his expression. What was the man implying? She didn't have issues of this magnitude with her mother.

"Bobby also confessed to planting the cell phone at Mateo's apartment," Matthew said.

Raina nodded. "Of course! He probably accessed their apartment when he stopped by to sell them rental insurance."

"How did you know?"

"Because he tried to do the same thing to me," Raina said. It seemed so obvious in hindsight. "What's going to happen to Detective Sokol?"

"Nothing. Youri is claiming stress leave."

"You're kidding me?"

"He's too stressed from filling in as the acting chief. And let's not forget, he's a new father with twin boys."

"Are you telling me he gets away with being a whack-a-do?" Raina asked, her voice full of incredulity. "I should walk around with a wallet full of baby pictures."

"The chief doesn't want to deal with it, especially with his impending retirement."

"I don't understand."

"First, there's all the documentation and paper-work to get rid of someone. And knowing Youri, he'll probably sue the department, so there will be even more paperwork and meetings with lawyers. You can't blame the chief for not wanting to deal with this in his last year."

"So Detective Sokol would become the next chief's problem."

Matthew nodded grimly. "Yeah, but it won't be my problem."

Raina wasn't so sure about this. Detective Sokol might be Matthew's headache. Everyone wanted him to be the next chief even if he didn't want it...yet.

"I need to finish the press release to retract the serial killer information this afternoon," Matthew said. "I hate cleaning up other people's messes."

They worked side by side for the next few minutes. Finally, Matthew glanced at the clock. It was almost four o'clock.

"That was a long break. When are they coming back to help?" Matthew asked.

"They're probably done for the day. The Early Bird Special at the Venus Cafe starts in five minutes," Raina said.

"Like I said, you're too easy."

Raina rolled her eyes. "Hey, you never told me which one of my cousins got engaged."

Matthew smiled, his eyes twinkling in amusement. "Your arch nemesis—Jung-yee. To a guy named Blue. I can't tell if that's a nickname or his real name."

Raina's face froze. Her cousin was engaged to her ex-boyfriend? The man who dumped her when she refused to move back to the Bay Area. She sneaked a glance at Matthew's face. He didn't know.

This was just fabulous. She would have to tell Matthew her history with the bridegroom before they visited the Bay Area again. With the millions of men out there, what were the odds her cousin would end up engaged to her ex? Did she do this intentionally to get back at Raina for a childhood slight?

"And she wants you to be one of her bridesmaids," Matthew said.

"You're kidding me."

"Her mother wants you to be a bridesmaid. You can't say no to your aunt."

"Oh, joy, joy," Raina said. She paused, running the timeline through her head. "I might be able to reject the offer. After all, I need to plan our wedding too."

Matthew slung an arm around Raina's shoulder. "Your mother already accepted on your behalf. Sorry, Rainy. Just think of this as practice for planning our wedding."

Raina sighed. She had planned plenty of large parties before at her grandma's side. What she needed was a lesson on how not to kill her cousin in the upcoming months.

THE END

PLEASE REVIEW my books at your *retailer*. As an indie author, reviews help other readers find my books. I appreciate all reviews, whether positive or negative.

Smoldering Flames and Secrets
(Raina Sun Mystery #7)
Don't miss the fun. Buy now.

Or meet Lucy Fong
Just Shoot Me Dead
(Lucy Fong Mystery #1)

ACKNOWLEDGMENTS

A story is a dream that a writer brings to life on paper. But a book needs a team to nurture it into an enjoyable experience.

I want to thank my editors, Alicia S. and Brandee, for wrangling my words so they are coherent.

And then, there are my beta-readers—Marion D., Joyce S., Cindy I., Della D., and Sharon S.—thank you, ladies, for volunteering your time to catch these sneaky typos and grammatical errors.

Thanks, readers Peaches La Farge, Michele LaForge (no they are not sisters), and Sandra Rankin for volunteering to be characters in my books. Also, thanks to service dog, Poe, for lending your name to a beast of a dog even though you're a sweetie.

And finally, thank you, Susan C. for the awesome cover.

I wouldn't have been able to bring this story to life without all of you.

—Anne R. Tan

ALSO BY ANNE R. TAN

Thanks for reading *Murky Passions and Scandals.* I hope you enjoyed it!

Want to know about new releases, sale pricing, and exclusive content?

Sign up for Anne R. Tan's email newsletter at http://annertan.com/newsletter

Your information would not be sold or transferred. Thank you for trusting me with your email.

Want More Raina Sun?

Raining Men and Corpses (Raina Sun #1)

Gusty Lovers and Cadavers (Raina Sun #2)

Breezy Friends and Bodies (Raina Sun #3)

Balmy Darlings and Death (Raina Sun #4)

Sunny Mates and Murders (Raina Sun #5)

Murky Passions and Scandals (Raina Sun #6)

Smoldering Flames and Secrets (Raina Sun #7)

Hazy Grooms and Homicides (Raina Sun #8)

Chilly Comforts and Disasters (Raina Sun #9)

Fair Cronies and Felonies (Raina Sun #10)

How about another series by Anne R. Tan?

Just Shoot Me Dead (Lucy Fong #1)

Just Lost and Found (Lucy Fong #1.5)

Just a Lucy Break-In (Lucy Fong #2)

EXCERPT FROM "SMOLDERING FLAMES AND SECRETS" (RAINA SUN MYSTERY #7)

As Raina Sun studied the groom—who was an ex-boyfriend—he continued to track her fiancé's movements under hooded eyes on the winery's lawn. The bridal party and a handful of family members loitered around the space and picked at the snacks set out for them, waiting for the call to be photographed with the bride and groom. The rolling green hills of the Livermore winery made a stunning backdrop for wedding photos, but Raina felt dread settling into her stomach.

Sebastian Luc, "Blue" to his friends, was dressed in his white tux with a turquoise bow tie. The color set off his hazel eyes, turning them into an arresting shade of blue with golden flecks among all the brown eyes in the bride's Chinese family. He flashed the deep dimple on his right cheek when he thanked the photographer and walked "off stage," leaving his bride, Raina's cousin, to pose by herself.

While his gaze scanned the crowd, his hand

brushed a lock of black hair off his forehead. As with all mixed race children, his height and Eurasian features looked exotic among the Wong family, like a peacock among a gathering of swans. His gaze locked in on Raina's fiancé again like a homing pigeon, and he made his way to join the men gabbing by the drinks cooler.

A hand waved in front of Raina's face. She blinked, breaking off her thoughts. She turned to Lucy Fong, her grandma's foster granddaughter. "I'm sorry. What did you say?" The two of them were sitting underneath the pop-up shade canopy on the lawn, a few feet away from the main crowd.

Lucy grinned at her. "Your wedding will come soon enough. You don't need to keep your eyes on your man. No one will steal him from under your nose at a family gathering."

Raina flushed. She wanted to march up to Blue and demand to know why he was marrying her cousin but watching her fiancé like a salivating dog. He wasn't gay, so why the sudden interest in Matthew? However, this would probably get her into more trouble than it was worth. "Did you ask me something?"

"I'm here if you want to talk about it," Lucy said.

Like the groom, Lucy was also half-Chinese. Her black hair was in a pixie cut with red streaks. The fringes of her bangs highlighted the brown eyes and delicate cheekbones of her heart-shaped face. Raina's foster cousin was close to five foot eight inches with her heels. Her hideous designer bridesmaid dress matched Raina's, but her height turned the geometric print on the ball gown into a thing of beauty.

On Raina, the dress added fifteen pounds to the hips. The bodice was full of daisies—the 3D kind that protruded from the fabric—and flattened what little chest she had. She would have looked more attractive walking around in a burlap sack and a Hawaiian lei. And to make her torment complete, all these outfits would have to be dry cleaned before show time next weekend, and it was her job to take care of it.

"There's nothing to talk about," Raina said, forcing a smile on her face.

From a distance, she could hear Gigi yipping. Her grandma was pet sitting the Boston terrier for an acquaintance. Unfortunately, the dog complained whenever she was within smelling distance of Raina. "I better go inside before Gigi's barking gets on everyone's nerves."

Before she could take a step toward the house, Gigi charged into the middle of the group, her leash dragging a lawn chair in her wake. When she looked behind her, there was panic in her face. As the dog ran to get away from the plastic chair, she crashed into bridesmaids and photo equipment alike.

Po Po, Raina's grandma, ran after the dog. "Gigi! Stop, girl. Stop."

"Holy Toledo," Lucy muttered, covering her mouth with a hand.

"We need to help Po Po," Raina said.

Lucy shook her head. "Not my monkey, not my circus." She didn't bother hiding the grin on her face.

Raina laughed. "You're so bad."

"Po Po would film the entire thing with her cell phone and post it up on YouTube. She's lucky I have restraint," Lucy said.

Gigi ran away from the patio and onto the lawn. The leash towed a lawn chair, tablecloth, and a watermelon fruit basket. The dog's tongue lolled out of her mouth. Her eyes were white with terror. Oh, the poor baby.

"We need to get the dog before my cousin has a hernia," Raina said, kicking off her heels and rushing toward the dog and her grandma.

Lucy followed her lead and soon over took Raina with her longer legs. They spread out, hoping to box the dog in with Po Po coming up from the rear.

"Somebody needs to get this dog off the lawn," Cousin Jung-yee shouted. Her reddened face and flashing brown eyes made Raina pick up her pace.

Gigi swiveled her head toward the bride. The dog made a wide arc on the lawn to change direction. Po Po lunged and slid like a baseball player to cut the dog off, but all she got for her effort was a face full of grass and the watermelon fruit basket. As the Boston terrier charged toward the bride, the plastic chair legs dug into the lawn and clumps of lush green grass followed in her wake.

Jung-yee's eyes widened. She grabbed the full skirt of her wedding dress to run away from the animal, but her three-inch heels got tangled on the train. She screamed as she fell to the ground. "Help—"

Before she could finish, Gigi was on Jung-yee. The dog pounced on the bride and licked her face. Gigi wiggled her tail so excitedly that her bottom got tangled in the tulle fabric around her. The lawn chair and tablecloth waited behind her like silent servants. While Gigi hated Raina, she loved Jung-yee with an equal passion. Too bad the love was unrequited.

The patio went silent. Po Po stopped short at the sight. She gave Raina a look of horror, changed direction, and fled back into the house.

Raina stopped running and tiptoed toward the disaster. She didn't want to spook the dog and have her blaze another trail of destruction. "Come here, Gigi. Be a good girl."

"Get her off of me!" Jung-yee said. "Get this beast off me." She pushed ineffectively at the dog.

Lucy trotted forward, scooped up the dog, unclipped the leash, and headed toward the house. "I'll keep Gigi out of everyone's hair," she said over her shoulder. Smart woman. If Jung-yee got her hands on the dog, there was no telling what would happen.

Raina and Blue got to the bride at the same time. Each of them took an arm and hauled her off the ground. Jung-yee was sobbing by this time. Her once sleek up-do was a tumbling mess around her face. Mascara ran down her cheeks. She was trembling, though Raina couldn't tell if it was from suppressed anger or defeat.

"It's okay. We'll have this cleaned up in no time," Blue said, wrapping his bride in his arms. He kissed her hair, but she continued to sob.

Raina untangled the train and brushed off the grass and dirt. Her cousin would have to change into her red Chinese dress for the rest of the photo shoot. As she straightened another section of the dress, her hands hovered over the fabric. There were red paw prints on the skirt.

Jung-yee pushed away from her fiancé, ran a finger under each eye—not that it helped—and straightened her back. "Bridget! Call the makeup and hair people. See if they can come back within the hour. Thank you." As the operations manager for her father's chain of Chinese restaurants, she was used to issuing commands. Though her voice wobbled, it didn't make her any less formidable.

Raina bent over the paw prints for a closer look. The liquid was thick and dried to a deep burgundy.

Jung-yee's gaze swept down to her skirt, and she grimaced. "I need a club soda before the stain sets." She brushed at it, and her fingers came away red. As her face changed from determination to horror, her hand trembled. "What…"

Raina swallowed. "It's blood."

Raina backed out of the sitting room, closing the door softly. She took a deep breath, thankful she was in the hallway instead of dealing with a weeping bride inside. She didn't blame her cousin for the meltdown, but she didn't want to get caught in the crossfire.

Even with the help of a wedding planner, the time and expense for planning a party for over four hundred guests was stressful. Chinese weddings were never a small event because the parents either had a large extended family or a network of friends and associates. Leaving someone off the guest list could be interpreted as a loss of face and start a family feud. And to top it off, the elders didn't believe in RSVPing for weddings. It was always a toss-up as to how many guests actually showed up. Everyone gave a red envelope filled with money to help offset the cost. If an absent guest forgot to send along a red envelope, the host family might take offense.

Politics were nothing compared to the intricacies surrounding a Chinese wedding, and the expectations between host and guest. Sometimes it had little to do with celebrating the love between a bride and groom. And with her cousin's perpetual need to be more Chinese than everyone else, the stress must be the size of Texas.

Raina sighed. Her poor cousin. Even though Jung-yee had spent their entire childhood competing in a one-sided match, Raina wouldn't wish this on her worst enemy. She hoped the cleaners would be able to remove the bloodstains. But where did the blood come from? Everyone looked hale and hearty. There was enough blood to look like someone had a stab wound.

She shivered at the unlucky thought and pushed it aside.

She smelled her fiancé's unique scent—a sage and clean water body wash—and spun around to find E. Matthew Louie approaching her. He was named after his father but went by his middle name. And after decades of calling her fiancé Matthew, she sometimes forgot he even had a different first name.

He was in a white tux with a silvery gray bow tie. As a courtesy to Raina, he was made a groomsman—an honor he had tried to get out of since day one. He had stayed away from the months of planning, but he had to make an appearance for the photo shoot this morning and the family dinner tomorrow.

His normally amused gold-flecked brown eyes were dark with concern. "How is Jung-yee doing?"

"She has calmed down a bit, but she's still weeping. Were you able to track down the source of the blood-stains?" she asked.

He shook his head. "The guys and I went through every inch of the front and back lawns and patio. The bridesmaids went through the event center. We couldn't find anything that would account for the bloodied paw prints." He raked a hand through his thick black hair. "We should broaden our search beyond the proximity of the building."

Matthew was a police detective in their small town of Gold Springs. He was also an ex-Marine who did side jobs for extra cash, though Raina didn't know his clients. She suspected one of them was her uncle, the criminal lawyer. Her fiancé approached an investigation methodically, leaving no stone unturned. There were times when Raina's spaghetti-on-the-wall approach drove him nuts.

"Did Gigi hurt herself running?" Raina asked.

He shook his head again. "I found Lucy with the dog in one of the small conference room. She cleaned Gigi's paws, and there was no trace of a wound."

Now this was even more intriguing. "Did you speak to Po Po?" Raina asked.

"No one has seen your grandmother. We tried calling her, but she's not picking up her cell phone."

Raina frowned. What if the blood came from her grandma? But Po Po had run rather vigorously after the dog.

As if following her train of thought, Matthew said, "I don't think so. Your grandma was too vivacious to be suffering from blood loss." He chuckled. "Did you see the way she tried tackling the dog?"

Raina grinned at the memory. The look on her grandma's face when she ended up with the watermelon fruit basket was priceless. "Has anyone checked the barn or wine cellar?"

"I don't even know where they are located. The winery is ninety acres."

"They're down the hill, beyond the first rows of grapevines. They process and bottle the grapes in the barn, and the wine is stored temporarily in the cavernous cellar underneath it. They also have two aging caves. They gave us a tour of the facility when we first checked out this venue."

Matthew looked at the heels on Raina's feet. "Do you want to change shoes before traipsing through the dirt?"

Raina wiggled her toes. If she and Matthew found the source of the blood, she wouldn't want to stain another dress. "Give me five minutes. I want to change into something more comfortable."

He grinned. "Do you need any help?"

"No, thank you. If someone is hurt, showing up an hour later isn't much help."

He wiggled his eyebrows. "Who needs an hour? I could get done in two minutes."

She rolled her eyes. "Yes, I'm familiar with *those* two minutes."

"Hey! Those were the best two minutes of your life."

She laughed. "If you say so."

Raina disappeared into the room next door, which was used as a dressing room by all the bridesmaids. She got into her regular clothes—a T-shirt and capris. It took her more than two minutes to get out of the dress.

When she stepped back into the hallway, Matthew glanced up from his cell phone. His face was ashen, and his lips were pressed into a thin line.

"What happened?" Raina asked, stepping up to her fiancé and wrapping an arm around his waist.

Matthew's frown became even grimmer. "Your

brother just texted me. One of the field hands found a body among the grapevines. Gigi's bloodied paw prints led the worker to the crime scene."

"Does anyone recognize the victim?"

He shook his head. "She wore a tank top and yoga pants. She wasn't an employee."

Raina blinked. And if the victim were a member of the owner's family, someone would have recognized her. "How did the woman die?"

"A single bullet between the eyes. She was executed."

Smoldering Flames and Secrets
Raina Sun Mystery #7
Don't miss the fun. Buy now.

ABOUT THE AUTHOR

Anne R. Tan is a *USA Today* bestselling author. She writes the Raina Sun Mystery series and the Lucy Fong Mystery series. Her humorous cozy mysteries feature Chinese-American amateur sleuths dealing with love, family, and life while solving murders.

Sign up for her newsletter for new release announcement, sales, and exclusive content at http://annertan.com/newsletter/

A Note from Anne:

My books are my legacy to my children. Unfortunately, they won't grow up in the San Francisco Bay Area as I did. Without a cultural hub to keep the language and philosophies alive, our family will lose this part of our heritage in one generation. My children will be visitors to this rich culture just like my readers. I hope you'll enjoy your time with Raina Sun and her large dynamic family.